DEATH BY
BABYSITTING

Acknowledgments

Thanks for technical assistance are due to Jeff Dykstra of Washington County (Pa.) Children and Youth Services and to Amy McGarrity, M.D. and St. Clair Pediatric Associates. Any technical errors or opinions expressed are of course entirely my own.

Dedication

To my parents, Paul and Alice (Zwick) Kimmel, who gave me a childhood I enjoy revisiting—a time and place full of wonderful characters, stories, laughter, and dreams.

DEATH BY BABYSITTING

SUSAN KIMMEL WRIGHT

HERALD PRESS
Scottdale, Pennsylvania
Waterloo, Ontario

Library of Congress Cataloging-in-Publication Data
Wright, Susan Kimmel, 1950-
    Death by babysitting / Susan Kimmel Wright.
     p. cm.
    Summary: As thirteen-year-old Nellie tries to solve the
mystery surrounding a baby left at her church nursery,
she gets some unexpected help from the dog her aunt
has recently adopted.
    ISBN 0-8361-3694-2
    [1. Abandoned children—Fiction. 2. Babies—Fiction.
3. Christian life—Fiction. 4. Mystery and detective
stories.]
    I. Title.
PZ7.W9587De 1994
[Fic]—dc20   94-11974
                                     CIP
                                     AC

The paper used in this publication is recycled and meets
the minimum requirements of American National Standard for Information Sciences—Permanence of Paper for
Printed Library Materials, ANSI Z39.48-1984.

DEATH BY BABYSITTING
Copyright © 1994 by Susan K. Wright
    Published simultaneously in Canada by Herald Press,
    Waterloo, Ont. N2L 6H7. All rights reserved
Library of Congress Catalog Number: 94-11974
International Standard Book Number: 0-8361-3694-2
Printed in the United States of America
Book design by Jim Butti/Cover art by Matt Archambault

1 2 3 4 5 6 7 8 9 10 00 99 98 97 96 95 94

Contents

DEATH BY BABYSITTING

1

Death by Babysitting

"Hey! Come back here!" Nellie grabbed at but missed one-year-old Toby as he streaked, diaperless, for the church nursery door.

Babysitting was just another miserable teenage problem. The older Nellie got, the more of those she was finding. She blew spiky red bangs out of her eyes. Maybe she should just give up trying to grow them out and go back to the Raggedy Ann look.

"Mommy!" Toby shoved at the door. Splinters stuck out of the top, where a hook had once been ripped out by another little darling in search of Mommy.

"Mommy's upstairs in a meeting, Toby." Nellie bent one arm around his waist and hauled him back to the changing pad, an old clown-printed crib mattress on the floor. "Let Nellie get a nice, dry diaper on you, and you'll see Mommy soon."

Nellie couldn't even hear herself over Toby's

screams. He rolled away before she got the first side of the diaper taped.

"Toby!" What a great Saturday afternoon. For a moment, Nellie actually yearned to be doing her math at the kitchen table.

"Nellie!" Peggy wailed from across the room. "Danny threw up."

"He does that all the time. Clean him up."

"He's *your* brother." Peggy's blue eyes were accusing. She had dark curls and a lap full of curdled baby formula. Being an only child, like Nellie had been for thirteen blissful years—she'd never had to face a five-month-old with a trick stomach.

"Which means it's your turn for a change," Nellie told her. "Hey, I've got my hands full already." She wrestled Toby to the floor.

A moment later, she raised her arms in victory. "Put me on the rodeo circuit," she said as Toby took off, clean diaper in place.

The Baltzer twins were fighting over a stuffed Dalmatian. The dog was losing. Polyester lava erupted over the shabby carpet and both red-faced toddlers.

"Oh, girls! Let go of poor doggie!"

Nellie headed toward the twins—but at the creak behind her had to change direction. Toby had made it through the door.

Begg City wasn't much of a town. In fact, it only had one traffic signal, on the corner by the courthouse. But people came from miles around to go to the Begg City Community Church.

In Nellie's humble opinion, the church was too big. Its nursery was a preschool room on weekdays, and ran nearly the length of the basement level of the church—as big as a parking lot. At Nellie's church, they had no nursery—and even if they had, there weren't ten hallways for babies to disappear into.

She caught Toby near the top of the steps. Familiar shrieks of an unhappy baby approached from behind.

She was surrounded. It was a nightmare—babies coming at her from everywhere.

Nellie turned around, clutching the struggling Toby. She glared down at her best friend.

"Peggy! You can't chase me with a baby that's all covered with spit-up."

Peggy was green in the dim light. "Nellie," she pleaded, "I have a very weak stomach."

Nellie pushed at her. "Go on back down. Everybody up there can hear us."

"All right. But please take care of Danny. I'll watch Toby."

"Sure, you will," Nellie muttered. "Now. After I changed a diaperload of toxic waste."

When they walked back into the nursery, though, she took her brother. Danny was already nearly as heavy as Toby, with skin the shade of light brown sugar and a cap of dark curls. He smelled of baby powder and sour milk.

She hadn't wanted a brother, hadn't wanted her parents to adopt a baby from Colombia. Nobody in Prescott County did that. But after two months, Danny was growing on her.

"Kind of like a fungus," she told him. He grinned toothlessly through a wreath of spit-up and stuffed a strand of her hair into his mouth.

Nellie whirled at the squeak of the outside door across the room. Not another escape artist!

But a wail came from the screened crib in that corner. Someone had just come in late and dropped off yet another baby.

Nellie sighed. She loved Danny, but she understood how a mom could get totally wiped out and want to dump little Junior or Tiffany on a pair of dumb thirteen-year-olds for an afternoon. Or maybe forever.

"I like the way everybody in youth group votes to help with the district meeting, and we end up alone in the nursery with ten kids." Peggy came from the bathroom grumbling, still mopping at her sweatshirt and jeans with a wet paper towel.

She slumped against the yellow-painted block wall as Toby ran off to fight for a mouthful of dog stuffing. On a poster above her, Jesus beamed, arms outstretched to gather a clean and happy flock of children. Nellie wondered if the artist really had a clue about little kids.

She turned Danny to face outward. "Nine kids," Nellie said, pulling her well-slimed hair out of Danny's mouth. "And Suzi's helping, too."

"Ten kids," Peggy told her. "And all Suzi's done is read to the bigger ones."

Suzi Rastetter sat in a rocker in the corner opposite the outside door, a peaceful nook sheltered by tall bookcases. Two kids, themselves almost old enough to help out, sat on the floor at her feet. Suzi's white-gold curls looked soft against the pale peach of her fuzzy sweater and stretch pants.

Peggy's martyred sigh turned into a smile. "After I break up the dog fight, I'm going to grab that screaming baby someone just dumped in the corner crib and give him to Suzi. I'm sure she wants to help, if she just knew what to do."

Nellie grinned. As if Peggy chose to be up to her armpits in anything nasty herself.

Nellie looked around, counting heads. There *were* ten children, she realized.

She frowned. It was scary. They were responsible for all these little kids and she wasn't even sure how many they had. Some of these parents had been a little too eager to drop off their kids and run.

Nellie wiped at Danny's face with a damp cloth as Peggy emerged from behind the crib screens. She carried the latest arrival, a tiny dark-haired girl in a pink sleeper who was still shrieking like a burglar alarm.

Walking over, Nellie glanced again at Suzi, who appeared lost in *The Poky Little Puppy*. She couldn't help admiring the girl's absolute concentration. With such an obvious appreciation for literature, Nellie wondered why Suzi couldn't get above a C in English.

"Who's this?" Nellie asked.

"I don't know." Peggy jiggled hopefully at the

baby, who only screamed harder. "Oh, Nellie! Nothing helps. She's dry. She doesn't want a bottle. She doesn't like to bounce."

Nellie looked at the clock, which still showed daylight savings time, and mentally subtracted an hour. "Well, the meeting should soon be over. You can hand her to her mother and run the other way."

"Don't worry. I will. I can't believe some people babysit every weekend." Peggy's eyes were wide with the horror of it all.

Nellie switched Danny to her other hip and gave her a look.

"Sorry. But you're good with babies. Hey!" Peggy's face brightened. "Maybe you can quiet her down."

Nellie backed away, clutching Danny like a human shield. "No thanks. That screeching's killing me."

Peggy rolled her eyes heavenward like Joan of Arc waiting for a light. "It got me already! Death by babysitting."

The stairway door creaked open.

"Restart your heart, Peg. Meeting's over."

Peggy's smile of relief was pitiful. "That was a close one." She glared at Suzi, who already had her JV cheerleader jacket on and was dashing toward the exit.

Nellie's parents were the first through the door. "Hi, girls!" Dad stepped cheerfully over scattered blocks and stampeding toddlers, lifting Danny from her arms. A man who came to church meetings dressed for barnwork never noticed a little clutter.

"Were you a good boy?" Mom asked.

Danny's arms flew up and down and he whacked her nose. Mom grabbed and kissed his fist. She looked around.

"Where did everybody go?"

"We were it," Peggy whined. "Three of us, if you count Suzi—but I wouldn't. And ten kids, Mrs. Locke!"

Around them, parents were scooping up their children. "Oh, girls, I'm sorry," Mom said. "I could have stayed to help."

"We survived," Nellie told her.

"Well, I can help you pick up, anyway." Mom began throwing toys into baskets, her handwoven cape sweeping the floor. She looked like a nomadic sheepherder in search of a flock.

"We'll go start the car," Dad said.

"Leave the baby here till it's warmed up," Mom told him. "There's snow in the air this afternoon."

Dad was already stuffing Danny into his snowsuit. "We're men, Kit. We can handle it."

Peggy's mother and father came in as Dad was leaving. Nellie loved her parents, but sometimes she envied Peggy, whose folks dressed and acted like normal human beings.

"Are you about ready?" Mr. Penwick asked.

Peggy and Nellie looked around the room. The parents had all collected their children. Everyone except the wailing bundle in Peggy's arms.

"Who's this?" Mrs. Penwick wondered.

"That's what we'd all like to know," Peggy muttered. "We never saw who dropped her off. Can you do anything with her, Mom?"

"I don't know." With a doubtful expression, Mrs. Penwick took the red-faced infant. "It's been a long time since I had a baby."

"She can't be more than six months old," Mom said, peering right into its furious little face and smoothing a hand over its fuzzy head. "Nellie, why don't you girls run upstairs and see if her mother got tied up talking to somebody."

Nellie was on her way. Anything to get away from that noise.

They could still hear it up in the sanctuary. It echoed faintly in the quiet of a room lit only by the soft red glow of the eternal light at the side of the altar. Dusk muted the colors of the stained-glass windows.

One pane near the bottom had been replaced with regular glass. Wiping it clear with her hand, Nellie stood and looked down at the parking lot. Only a handful of cars remained. Except for a van that said Begg City Community Church on the side, and sat in one corner with its wheel off, the cars belonged to people she knew.

"Everybody's gone," Peggy said, with her talent for reporting the obvious.

Mothers don't just disappear, Nellie sternly told herself. The mother just misplaced her somehow.

They stood a moment, listening to the settling

16

sounds of the building, to the muffled cries from the room below, to the sound of their own breathing. Nellie's chest hurt with the effort to control her growing panic.

This long, miserable day was supposed to be *over*. It was time to go home. What were they supposed to do with that squalling baby?

Wordlessly, she walked up the aisle, Peggy at her heels. Their steps shushed on the carpet as they checked every pew. Maybe the baby's mother was catching a nap—or hiding from the noise.

They found two pens and a crumpled tissue. No mothers.

2

Abandoned!

"We're dead meat," Peggy groaned as they returned downstairs after searching the rest rooms. "We lost an entire mother."

"We didn't lose anybody. She lost herself," Nellie snapped. "She probably just forgot to pick up the baby."

Peggy paused at the nursery door to give Nellie a look. "Nobody *forgets* a baby."

"Dad forgot Mom and me at the mall," Nellie told her. "Twice."

Peggy just shook her head.

"Okay," Nellie admitted. "Bad example." Some days it was a miracle Dad remembered to chew.

"No point putting it off." Nellie reached around Peggy and shoved the door open.

"They're going to say it's our fault," Peggy predicted. "We don't even know who she is."

Nellie blinked in the sharp brightness of the room. There were more people standing around now, faces white and strained in the fluorescent light. The baby's screams probably had something to do with that. She'd cried so long she was half-gasping and hiccuping with each howl.

Mom held her now. Dad and Danny were back inside. So were the Rastetters, a man Nellie recognized as the Community Church pastor, and the Kepplers.

A thin man in glasses came in the opposite door. "The police are on the way," he said.

Nellie heard Peggy's moan behind her. *Police.*

She looked across the room, trying to catch Rick Keppler's eye. He was listening to something Suzi was telling him, though, his dark head bent close to her clump of yellow frizz.

Now Nellie knew why Suzi had been in such a hurry to get outside. She'd been hanging around the parking lot, flirting with Rick.

Nellie wasn't jealous. Rick liked Nellie—she knew that. But she started walking over anyway.

"Nellie." Dad motioned her.

Nellie looked over at Rick. He glanced up and smiled. That smile always made her grin like a fool, even at the worst of times.

Reluctantly, she went to see what Dad wanted. Peggy trailed after her.

Dad put his hand on Nellie's shoulder. "Nellie, this is Pastor Weimer. Do you girls have any idea at all who left this baby here? Pastor Weimer may be able to recognize a description."

Nellie swallowed. It seemed she was always the center of attention—for all the wrong reasons. She shook her head. "One minute we had eight kids. A minute later there were nine—I mean ten."

"When did you first notice the baby?" Pastor Weimer was a big man with kind eyes and a soothing voice.

"A little while before the meeting broke up. Peggy was in the bathroom, cleaning off her clothes, and I was turned the other way. The door kind of squeaked shut, and I turned around. There she was. Just crying and crying." Nellie pointed at the crib near the parking lot door.

"I first noticed her when the twins were ripping up the dog," Peggy said.

"Stuffed dog," Nellie explained, seeing eyebrows go up.

"It was like everything was happening at once," Peggy said. "And there were only two of us." She glared in Suzi's direction.

"When was that?" Mom asked.

"Maybe fifteen minutes before everybody came down," Peggy said.

"Did anybody ask Suzi?" Nellie nodded in her direction. "She was here, too. Reading to the big kids."

"I don't know," Dad admitted, running a hand through his hair. "We're kind of disorganized."

"Could everyone please gather around?" Pastor Weimer called out in a pulpit voice.

Rick ambled over, hands in his hip pockets. He shoved Nellie with one shoulder. "Hey."

"Hi, Rick." Her heart lifted like a kite caught

on an updraft. With his solid warmth beside her, Nellie relaxed a little.

"While we're waiting for the police, we need to figure out what we know about this little one." Pastor Weimer glanced at the baby, who'd finally sobbed herself to sleep on Mom's shoulder.

"You're Suzi?" he asked. "Did you happen to notice when the baby was dropped off?"

She shook her head. "I was busy trying to entertain those bigger kids and keep them out of trouble." Her violet gaze slid from Nellie to Peggy. "They couldn't seem to handle the babies over there. It was so wild and noisy that one more or less—" She shrugged, pretty and apologetic.

Nellie itched to give her a smack, but Pastor Weimer, not to mention Suzi's parents, probably wouldn't appreciate it.

"Who was parking cars?" the minister asked.

Rick pulled a hand out of his pocket and raised it. "I was. And Chris, our youth group adviser."

"Were you there the whole time?"

"We did stick around," Rick said, "since some people needed to leave early, and we had them blocked in. But I wasn't outside the whole time. It was so chilly we took turns warming up inside the front door."

"Did you notice anyone go in with a child and not bring her out again afterward?" Pastor Weimer asked.

Rick shook his head. "It was getting dark and the lot was so jammed. I'm sorry."

21

A buzzer sounded, making Nellie jump. The thin man headed for the stairs. "That's the front door. The police must be here."

Rick turned and took Nellie's icy hands. "You okay?"

She managed a shrug, but tears shoved at her eyelids. "We tried so hard," she told him. "There were just too many kids."

"I know." He smoothed a hand over the back of her head, like Mom had done to the baby. "Nobody's saying it was your fault."

"We're going to be in trouble," Peggy moaned. "You wait and see." Her eyes got big. "What if they don't find the mother at all? Are we going to have to take that kid home with us?"

"Nah!" Nellie said encouragingly, even though she wasn't all that sure. "Hey, look on the bright side." Nellie tried to smile. "Nobody will ever ask us to babysit again."

Peggy buried her face in her hands.

The police came in and began working their way around the room, talking to everyone in turn. Nellie and Peggy had the pleasure of being first.

"Show us where you found the baby." The dark-skinned officer was all business, like a voice on the police radio.

"Over there." Peggy gestured with a jerky hand. She trotted after him like a puppy in obedience class. "Hey, we're really sorry. All of a sudden, there was the baby. I feel like if we'd been watching—I mean we *were* watching, but—"

22

Nellie hurried after them. The way Peggy collapsed in the presence of authority figures, she'd soon be confessing she and Nellie had kidnapped the baby.

The officer looked around the battered white nursery crib. He jotted something down and turned to the girls. "In here?"

Peggy nodded vigorously. "Right there." She pointed. "She was crying and crying and I—"

"Miss?" The officer raised a hand. Was there a glimmer of a smile in his eyes?

Peggy stopped, gulping for breath.

"Was there anything with her?" he asked. "A bag or anything?" He nudged with one knuckle at a nearly furless gray-white lamb.

"That lamb belongs here, I think," Peggy said. "But I'm not sure."

She looked around. "There wasn't any bag. Just a paper diaper and a bottle with formula in it."

"Where?"

Peggy pointed with a toe at the floor beneath the crib. "I don't know where they went."

"Maybe by the changing pad," Nellie suggested.

The bottle was still over there. "Anyone else handle this?"

Peggy shook her head. "I don't think so."

"Diaper?"

"I'm not sure. They all look alike to me. But that's the only one here, so that's probably it."

The officer wrote something.

"You know what was so bad?" Peggy said. "Everybody voted to help out but nobody came but us. There should've been at least two more people here. And with everybody crying—ow!"

She gave Nellie a dirty look. Nellie smiled an apology. It had just been a teeny little kick.

"I'm sure it was rough." The officer's voice had softened. Maybe in appreciation for Peggy's performance.

"It wasn't our fault," Peggy continued. "Well, a little bit, maybe. I mean, it was our job, but it's not like—" She eyed Nellie and shut up.

"Come over here, girls." The officer motioned them back to the center of the room.

Nellie looked at the baby, still sleeping in Mom's arms, its face tear-streaked. Its chest rose and fell in little puffs.

The poor little thing. Where was its mother? Surely she wouldn't really have abandoned it. What if something had happened to her? But how? What could be safer than a church meeting?

Pastor Weimer had produced a list of people at the meeting, but he admitted it probably wasn't complete. At least it gave the police a place to start.

Nellie slid in next to Rick again. "I heard them say the labels were cut out of the baby's clothes," he whispered, scraping back a dark forelock that fell across his eyebrow as he leaned down.

Nellie sucked in her breath. "You mean like somebody actually abandoned that baby and didn't want to be traced?" How could anyone ever do that?

Rick shook his head slightly, dislodging the same lock of hair. "Maybe. Sometimes people just cut them out because they're scratchy."

After adopting Rick, his parents had given birth to four more little boys, so he knew more about little kids than Nellie did. And she was only half-joking when she told him he was the one with all the maternal instinct. Nellie was a lot more comfortable with animals than babies.

A strong-looking woman arrived wearing black and white ski clothes that matched her streaked hair. She pulled a draft of cold air into the room with her and Nellie shivered.

"Meredith Piasecki," she told the police. "Children and Youth Services."

Nellie edged closer, trying to overhear their conversation. With everyone else in the room talking, it was hopeless. Peggy's chattering at her back didn't help.

"They're going to blame us," Peggy said. "I could tell the way he was questioning us."

"Shhh." Nellie went to stand beside Mom, who was talking to the Piasecki lady.

Mom ran her free hand gently along the baby's right leg. The baby grimaced in its sleep. "I'd get it checked by a doctor," Mom said. "The way it was crying wasn't normal. And this leg seems swollen."

Ms. Piasecki looked sharply at Nellie. "This girl found the baby?"

Mom nodded. She introduced the girls.

"I'm sure someone will soon be talking to you further," the woman said.

The baby looked so tiny as Mom placed it in the social worker's arms. "Where are you taking her?" Mom asked.

"Since no parent has come forward, we're taking the child into protective custody. She'll spend the night in an emergency foster home."

"Hey, she's welcome to stay with us," Dad offered, making Nellie groan in disbelief. "We've got lots of room."

Ms. Piasecki seemed to eye his shaggy hair and worn jeans. She shook her head. "Foster homes have to be approved in advance. We have a list. We can't put an infant in just any home."

Especially, Nellie thought, *with people who lose mothers, can't stop babies from crying and don't even know how many kids they're to be watching.* She hung her head like her dog Lady did when she'd been scolded.

Over in the corner, Suzi Rastetter's voice fell into a lull in all the talking. She was looking Nellie's way as the policeman wrote in his book.

"I took the Red Cross babysitting course, so I guess I ought to have been put in charge," Suzi said. "They should have had people sign in, but I doubt those two knew what they were doing."

Suzi sighed, a soft breath that carried across the now quiet room. "Well, I suppose we should be grateful none of the children actually got hurt. Babysitting is such a big responsibility."

3

Wanted by the Police for Questioning

Nellie ate another handful of chips and green onion dip and washed it down with cola. First those wild kids this afternoon, then the police—it had all left her stomach churning. Even junk food didn't seem to help.

On any other day, the housewarming would have been a nice party. Aunt Paula danced around her crowded living room with a tray of stuffed mushrooms that bounced like babies.

Nellie shook her head. It was time to relax.

"Mushroom?" Aunt Paula asked, her mossy green eyes checking Nellie's.

"No thanks." Nellie tried to smile. "I'm already as stuffed as they are."

Paula balanced the tray against her hip. "What do you think of the house, Nell?"

"I love it." Compared to their cluttered, falling-down farmhouse, Aunt Paula's place was gorgeous. It was a small Victorian with a fili greed porch, on the main road through Chestnut Grove. Paula had decorated it so it made you feel you were in an old-fashioned parlor.

The curved-backed couch was covered in eggplant-colored velvet and scattered with needlework pillows and heavy lace doily things. Paula's radio was in a big, polished oak case. It sat on a table surrounded by a jungle of green plants and antique porcelain animals.

"My friends think I'm becoming a real small-town girl," Paula said with a grin. Most of her guests came from Pittsburgh, where Paula had lived until recently. A lively bunch, they were mostly single like Paula and all talked at once.

"Some of them drove straight through town before they even knew it." She teasingly elbowed the bearded man next to her and he put on an indignant look.

"You said you lived in *town*," he complained. "Where I come from, that means more than ten houses at a crossroad."

"Actually, there are almost twenty," Paula pointed out.

"And sidewalks."

"There's a sidewalk out there, Bob," she insisted. "At least on this side of the road."

He patted her arm. "It takes more than a half-dozen cracked slabs with grass growing out of them before I'd call it a sidewalk," Bob said. "But it's real cute, anyway. If you can keep from being bored out of your gourd."

Aunt Paula just grinned again. "You'd be surprised at what's teeming under the surface in a small town."

Rick plopped down next to Nellie. He was holding a plate of meatballs and cheese puffs. "Great party, ma'am."

Nellie smiled. She loved how he always called Paula that.

"Thanks, Rick. And thanks for helping me paint last weekend."

"No sweat. It was kind of fun with everybody working together."

"Won't you miss your apartment?" Nellie asked. "You're going to be all alone here."

Paula tilted her head. For the hundredth time, Nellie wished she'd inherited Paula and Mom's looks instead of Dad's strong features. "Well, I've been thinking about that. I'll see people all day at the bookstore. But I think I'd like a dog to keep me company at night. I'm planning to run over to the shelter after work tomorrow."

"Be careful," Bob warned. "Unless it's a puppy, you don't know what you're getting. It could've been abused or just plain vicious. I know somebody who got a real wacko dog that way."

"Paula!"

At the voice from the kitchen, she turned. "Gotta go. Eat up, kids."

Half a step away, she added, "Don't worry anymore about today, Nellie." She tapped a cross-stitched sampler on the wall, then darted off.

Rick read the quotation from the book of Daniel. " 'Surely your God is the God of gods, and

the Lord of kings and a revealer of myster-
ies. . . .' "

Nellie sank back on the cushions. It wasn't
easy sitting around waiting for God to reveal
things. Not when in God's time a thousand years
were like a few hours. And not when people like
Suzi were blaming you for what happened.

"I wish Peggy would get here," she grumbled.
"There must be something we noticed that
would help. We just need to talk about it."

Rick shoveled a handful of cheese puffs into
his mouth and wiped his fingers. He was shaking
his head. "I doubt it," he finally said as he loaded
chips onto his plate.

"Nobody in the place seemed to remember a
thing. Face it," he told her. "There were a couple
hundred people there, and a bunch of kids. You
could've come in dressed like the bride of Kong
and dropped off a baby gorilla."

Nellie took another gulp of cola, carefully an-
gling her face away from Mom and Dad. They
were hanging out at the raw vegetable tray and
had suggested once or twice that she might do
the same.

Out of the corner of her eye, she saw Dad wave
a slice of sweet potato at her. She shuddered.
There was definitely such a thing as overdoing
those good eating habits.

"Do you think there were *any* suspects on
that list of Pastor Weimer's?" Nellie asked.

"Maybe." The way he said it meant "no." "He
knew most of the people on there, or someone

else did. So it was easy to run down the list and cross off the ones without babies."

"But there were some people from out of town," Nellie reminded.

"Some."

The doorbell rang; Aunt Paula pushed through the crowd to answer it. The Penwicks stood spotlighted under the porch lamp.

Nellie jumped up, with Rick behind her. She couldn't hear what they were telling Paula, but something was wrong.

Straining her ears over the rumbling and cackling of too many voices, she excused her way toward the door. Peggy met her eyes, looking like a cornered guinea pig.

Mr. Penwick was gesturing for Mom and Dad to come over. He looked as grim as Peggy.

"What's up, Curt?" Dad took Mr. Penwick's hand in both of his.

"The police just called. They want to see the girls down at the station in Begg City tomorrow."

Nellie's glance shot to Dad's face. He put his hand on her shoulder.

"They had the baby examined," Mrs. Penwick said. "It—she has a broken leg."

Dad stood behind Nellie now, hands on both her shoulders. She couldn't see his face, but his grip tightened.

"They didn't say so," Mr. Penwick said. "But they obviously think the baby was abused."

4

The Mystery Couple

Nellie looked at Rick. His mouth was hard and his eyes darker than ever.

Peggy's tears spilled out over her cheeks. "They're going to say it was us, Nellie. That we were stressed out and hurt the baby."

"Oh, Peggy, surely not." Mom reached out to smooth her hair. "Nobody's going to believe that."

Nellie stepped away from Dad's hands. "Don't be so sure. Suzi was telling anybody who'd listen that we were out of control in there."

"Let's not jump to conclusions, girls." Dad's voice was firm. "I may just be an equipment tech, but we see enough abuse cases at the hospital to know the pattern. Kids get abused by people who spend a lot of time cooped up with them—parents mostly. You girls were only in that nursery for a couple hours."

"And if you'd had a problem," Paula added,

"you could have just gone upstairs for help. You had no reason to lose your temper to that extent."

She smiled and started taking the Penwicks' coats. "Why don't you come in and get some food? That always makes things look brighter."

Peggy couldn't eat, though, and suddenly neither could Nellie. Some kids never seemed to get in trouble, but she and Peggy weren't like that. They could be doing something *good*—like helping in the nursery—and still end up blamed for something that wasn't their fault.

They slumped on the couch next to Rick, chins resting on their chests. Rick had squeezed three meatballs onto a frilled toothpick and aimed them at his mouth. Out of the corner of her eye, Nellie watched him.

"What if they ask a trick question and I say the wrong thing?" Peggy said. "We're going to have a police record."

"Oh, come on," Rick said. "They're not out to trick you. They probably just need more information."

Nellie gave him a sour look. "Did you ever read Agatha Christie? When they say someone's 'assisting the police in their inquiries,' it means he's the main suspect."

"That's England," Rick said, spearing meatballs. "Back in the old days, not now. This is the U.S. They won't work you over if you're going to be arrested. Not without reading you your rights."

"That'll help just bunches," Nellie said dryly.

Rick threw down his meatball-kabob. "Use your brain, Nellie."

He shook her shoulder, fixing her with dark eyes. "If they were going to arrest you, they'd have done it. If they even thought you had some hot info, they wouldn't be waiting till tomorrow. You girls always think everything revolves around you. Everything's got to be a big mystery, and you've got to solve it."

Nellie pushed him away, but she did feel a little better. What he said made sense. "Well, maybe we're not going to be arrested. But it *is* a big mystery. Wouldn't it be neat if we could find the baby's mother? Then we'd be heroes."

Rick rolled his eyes toward the ceiling and went back to his plate of goodies. Nellie and Peggy looked at each other. "Maybe we could match up people we do know that left off kids," Nellie said at last.

It didn't take long. Danny and the Baltzer twins were from their own church. By the time they got to the end of the list, there were only two babies they couldn't match with a parent. One of them was the abandoned baby.

Rick had been following their descriptions. Suddenly he sat up. "Hey, am I a dope. I did forget something. There was a couple that came in late. The lot was already pretty full.

"Chris was parking a car and I was holding back the next two. A woman got out of the second car, carrying a bundle into the downstairs.

34

Next time I noticed, the car was gone. I figured he parked it himself, along the street."

"Could they have just turned around and left without your knowing?" Nellie asked.

He shifted his glance to the chip bowl. "Yeah. Back right out onto the road and take off. I was looking around for spots where we could squeeze in another car," he explained. "And I don't think Chris would have seen them at all."

"It wasn't near the end of the meeting, was it?" Nellie tried not to hope.

Rick shook his head. "But if she was really planning to abandon the kid, she might have been waiting somewhere inside for the right moment."

Nellie ached with discouragement. "But the car disappeared right away."

"She could've left on foot, don't forget."

"What did they look like?" Peggy leaned forward, her fingers gripping the velvet of the couch seat.

Rick sank back, eyes closed in thought. He rolled his head slowly from side to side.

"Can't remember the driver. It was just too dark—light reflecting off the windshield.

"The lady was average-looking. Brown coat, I think. Light hair." He gestured at his shoulders for length. "Glasses? Maybe. I'm not a hundred percent on that."

Peggy looked hopefully at Nellie. Nellie shook her head.

Peggy's mouth sagged. "This is great," she said

at last. "They slipped *two* babies in on us without our even noticing. We *should* be arrested."

"I know." Nellie felt agreeable now that they had a lead, even if it wasn't much. "But maybe Suzi saw that woman. It's worth checking."

Peggy didn't budge from her disgusted slouch. "Get real. She was in a total coma over *The Poky Little Puppy.*"

"Hey," Nellie said. "She told the police it was noisy, so she must have had at least a few seconds of consciousness."

"Well, we'd better hope she had one of them when that woman in brown brought the baby in."

5

A Visit from the Police

Nellie winced, reading the article in the Monday morning Begg City *Bulletin*. That wasn't unusual, since the *Bulletin* didn't waste money on a proofreader. Counting typos was good breakfast table entertainment, especially when you came across an ad for "chicken barbecued over a blazing tire."

This morning Nellie wished there had been a big mistake to distract people. Unfortunately, everything in this article was spelled perfectly.

She winced because it reported a female infant had been abandoned Saturday at the Begg City Community Church nursery, which had been supervised by "three apparently inattentive teenage girls." At least it had said "three." Suzi would love being included in their little group.

It must have been a slow news day. Nellie had made the front page, along with a local hog farmer who was raising a contender for Grand Champion at the Pennsylvania Farm Show.

"Oh, Mom, this is horrible."

Mom was busy, mopping at Danny's unending drool stream. It had been a restless night for all of them with his teething. Mom didn't turn around. "Oatmeal's good for you. Just don't eat the burned spots."

"Not the oatmeal! This article about the baby. It says we were careless."

Mom turned in dismay. "Oh, Nellie, surely not. They wouldn't put that in a news article."

Nellie gave the paper a rough shove in Mom's direction. It caught a stack of junk mail and school papers, sprawling them across the table.

"This is the *Bulletin,* Mom. They do things their own way."

Mom pushed rumpled, dark-red hair behind her ears and began reading. A minute later, she looked up with a smile. "Well, that's not so bad. It doesn't really say you were careless."

"It says 'inattentive.' " Nellie's voice rose.

"Well, yes. But I think they're just saying you were—maybe distracted. I think they're just explaining how a baby can be dropped off without any of you noticing."

Mom's version didn't sound a whole lot better. "Really, we weren't careless," Nellie told her. "That's a big room and there were too many kids and not enough of us. We really did try."

Nellie's voice trailed off. She was whining like Peggy.

"Everyone knows you did, sweetie." Mom gave her a little hug. "Here, take your lunch or you'll miss the bus."

Nellie took the crumpled brown bag. She collected her hat and gloves that had been warming on the shelf above Mom's old-fashioned wood cookstove.

Mom was smart. She'd taught high school English before Danny arrived. But she never gave a thought how people talked. She cooked over a wood fire in the age of car phones and VCR's. She fixed tofu salad sandwiches with alfalfa sprouts and expected Nellie to eat them openly in the school cafeteria.

Mom laid a kiss on Nellie's cheek and pulled the door open to a gust of air that smelled of rotting logs and wet leaves. "At least the policeman yesterday made it pretty clear they don't think you and Peggy hurt the baby. When they locate her parents, no one's going to give you another thought." She gave Nellie a little shove and closed the door behind her.

Nellie pulled her collar up around her neck, trying to thwart the wind. Winter was blowing in on that wind, a bit more each day. It moaned through the woodlot on the hill, scouring the old, worn stones in the little graveyard just below the tree line.

When the wind reached Lockes' rundown farmhouse below, it stretched icy fingers into every gap and crack, trying as it had for a hundred winters past to tear the old house down.

At the sight of Nellie, Lady burst from the barn door to drive her like a reluctant lamb toward the bus stop. Nellie buried a gloved hand in the mixed-collie's ruff, getting an insulating layer of dog hair into the fiber.

Lady's breath rose in a cloud from her widely grinning face. "What's so funny?" Nellie grumbled.

Lady barked and spun in a circle, happy to be noticed.

Nellie stepped faster. The sound of the bus, struggling up the potholed road, made Lady switch to guard-dog mode. She charged snarling down the driveway in her daily attempt to protect Nellie from the bus's jaws.

Today of all days Nellie was rooting for the dog. But as always the bus lurched to a stop that looked like it might be its last. It tilted to starboard on the uneven road. The door opened.

Lady still barked valiantly, even though Nellie was clearly going to get on. Nellie guessed a dog on a bad road in the middle of nothing but overgrown fields needed to make its own excitement.

The bus turned in the driveway while Nellie worked her way to her usual seat at the back. Kathy Bauer half-turned as she went by. "Hey, bean brain. Suzi says you and Penwick really did it now. Nobody will give you another babysitting job till you're eighty-five."

"Big loss," Nellie muttered and kept walking.

"I heard that!" Kathy yelled after her. "I make twenty-five dollars a week babysitting, and when

I'm sixteen, I'm buying a car."

And that's where she probably was last weekend, Nellie thought. Someone was paying her twenty-five dollars to do what Nellie did for free—and the chance to be interrogated by the police. Maybe Kathy was right. Quite possibly she *was* a bean brain.

"Hi, Nell." Rick smiled as she slid in across the aisle from him and his friend, Fred Umbaugh.

Nellie's "Hi" turned into a yawn.

"Rough night?" Fred asked.

She nodded, dumping her books on the seat. "First I couldn't stop thinking. Then Danny started wailing, and he's right in the next room."

"Did the cops give you a hard time?" Rick asked.

Nellie shook her head. "No, you were right. They were just trying to squeeze out of us any little tidbit we might have forgotten."

"And did they?"

Nellie made a face. "There's nothing there to squeeze. I wish there were."

"Did you tell about the couple who came late?"

"Well, yeah. But you did, too, didn't you?"

"Sure. They spent about an hour with me, and that's really the only lead I could give them."

"Maybe the police will track them down today," Nellie said. "But then what? If it's their baby, will they get her back?"

"I don't think so. At least not right away."

"Did the police talk about abuse?" she asked.

"Not to me."

They hadn't said anything to Nellie, either, and she wondered if the baby really was abused. Maybe she'd just fallen down. But then why had she been left behind like an empty lunch bag?

Sleet was falling when the bus pulled into line at the school entrance. It made starry globs of slush on the steamed windows.

"Looks like you guys got company," Fred said, rubbing a spot on the glass.

Rick turned, and Nellie strained to see where Fred was pointing. A Begg City police cruiser was parked across the drive and just ahead of them.

Even being fairly sure she wasn't a suspect, Nellie felt her stomach start to polka. Since they weren't in Begg City, Fred was probably right. The police would be looking for Rick or the "three inattentive teenagers."

She gathered her books, dropping a ring binder from the clumsy armload. Rick picked it up, stuffing papers back inside, and slid it on top the heap.

He smiled, warm and slow like the sun coming up. Being visited by the police didn't seem to bother him, but then nobody had called him inattentive, either.

A smooth-faced young policeman met them on the sidewalk. He looked like he was playing dress-up in his uniform, like someone in the senior class play. He raised his brows.

"Rick Keppler?"

"Yes, sir."

"Would you come to the school office with me, please? We need you to identify someone for us. They don't live far from the school, so we figured we'd save you all a trip to the station."

Nellie and Rick exchanged a look. She shifted her books. "I'm Nellie Locke. Maybe I can help."

The officer only hesitated briefly. "All right. Maybe so. Come on along."

Fred gave them a thumbs-up and headed for class with his slow, stiff gait—the result of a farming accident years back that had cost him a leg. Nellie trailed after Rick, scanning the other buses in the lineup. Peggy's wasn't there.

When they got to the office, Nellie found herself swallowing. It was a small school, the same one she'd started in as a kindergartner. Something of the principal's scary reputation from those days still hung in the air, along with the smell of lemon furniture polish.

Now Nellie knew there wasn't a paddling machine in the back room. But she also realized there were worse punishments than a spanking.

The policeman nodded at Bonnie Hoffmann, sitting at the nearest typewriter. She'd only graduated last spring, and Nellie had trouble thinking of her as Miss Hoffmann.

Rick and Nellie trailed past Bonnie's desk, which was decorated with a wilting African violet and an empty candy dish, to a door marked "Assistant Principal." Indian Camp School had never had an assistant principal, so somebody had obviously been dreaming big. The room was used for conferences and for storing boxes of supplies.

The officer pushed open the door. A thin, balding man and rosy-faced woman looked up from a battered table in the middle of the room. The woman was holding a baby built like a pocket-size Sumo wrestler.

"Mr. and Mrs. D'Arrigo? Thanks for waiting. This is Rick Keppler and Nellie Locke."

He looked at Rick and Nellie. "Do either of you recognize the D'Arrigos?"

"I'm not sure," Rick admitted, still standing by the door. "They could be the couple I saw on Saturday."

Nellie collapsed a little inside, feeling hope ooze away. "I'm pretty sure I remember the baby," she said.

Most babies this age seemed to have at least two chins, but the D'Arrigo baby had four she could see from across the room. That tended to identify him, all right.

"Does he have a rash?" she asked, wondering if she'd have to look.

Mrs. D'Arrigo nodded, tears in her eyes. "He's allergic to the detergent I'd been using."

Nellie looked at the officer. "I'm pretty sure," she repeated.

Mr. D'Arrigo shifted in his chair and his wife turned red all the way to the roots of her sandy hair. "We're so sorry," Mrs. D'Arrigo said, hugging her baby.

She looked at them, eyes darting, then back at

44

the baby's cap of brown curls. "We know we shouldn't have done it, but we just needed a break so badly."

Mr. D'Arrigo gave a quick, nervous smile. "Ronny's been teething, and he has that rash. He just doesn't sleep. Becky was at her wits' end."

"It wasn't fair to you," Mrs. D'Arrigo admitted. "We should've just hired a sitter. But there was that meeting, and free babysitting—"

"And we just decided, let's go out to dinner," the man said. "We figured, what's the harm? It'll do us good."

"We never dreamed we'd cause so much trouble," his wife said. "We'll never do it again," she promised, eyes brimming.

"All right, kids," the officer said. "You can go to class. Miss Hoffmann will give you permission slips for being late. Thanks for your help."

Out in the hall again, Nellie looked at Rick. "There went the only lead we had."

6

Studio Wrestling— Cafeteria Style

Nellie sat at the end of the lunch table, tearing her sandwich into tiny pieces. She ate one. Bean spread on homemade bread was easier to get away with if people couldn't tell what it was and make faces.

Peggy slid her brown bag onto the table opposite Nellie. "Cold pizza?" she asked. "I've got extra."

Gratefully, Nellie slipped her bean debris back into the bag and crumpled it up. "Thanks."

"Did the policeman tell you anything?"

Nellie shook her head. "Only that there would be a custody hearing this afternoon. But that was on the news last night and this morning, anyway."

She peeled off a strip of cheese and began feeding it into her mouth. It was stiff, like plastic that had melted, then cooled.

"People have been so obnoxious," Peggy complained. "They think it's funny. 'Lost something, Penwick?' 'Hey, Penwick, babysit me—I want my parents to disappear!' "

Nellie groaned. "I know." She put down her pizza. "Lou Cascio said if they don't find the mother, we're going to be legally responsible for the baby."

Peggy went white around the mouth. "What?"

"I think he just wanted to scare me," Nellie said, bracing her elbow on the table and leaning her head against her fist.

"When you're legally responsible, does that mean you go to jail?"

"I don't think so. I think it just means it's like *you're* the mother. You have to pay for everything the baby needs and you have to raise her."

Peggy chewed her lip. "Now I'll never get another cat. Mom and Dad are going to kill me.

"Please, Nellie," she begged, "You've got a bigger house. Do you think your folks would let the baby live with you? I'll give you all my allowance and any money I earn."

"How are you going to earn anything?" Nellie snorted. "Nobody's going to hire you to babysit."

Peggy put her face in her hands. "I'm only thirteen, and now I'm stuck with a baby."

Nellie shook Peggy's shoulder. "Hey, Peg, come on. I told you I think Lou was just trying to shake me up."

Peggy's stricken eyes looked out from between her hands. "What if he wasn't, Nellie? His dad's a lawyer. Maybe he knows."

"Peggy, look. The social worker told me that they only put kids in approved homes. They have a list."

Peggy made a sour face. "They're also having a custody hearing today. What do you think that's for?"

"I don't know." Nellie stuffed the uneaten pizza into the bag along with her mangled sandwich. "But if it had anything to do with us, they'd tell us."

Peggy just sat and shook her head. "You don't have to live with the baby, anyway, to have to pay child support," she said darkly. "Think about it."

A shadow fell over the table. Suzi Rastetter stood beside them, clenching her fists at her sides. There were tears in her eyes.

"I just wanted to thank you two goof-ups for ruining my life."

Suzi wore eye makeup, and it had collected in tiny mud puddles under each eye. "I'm a good babysitter. I took a course and everything. And now, thanks to you, everybody's making fun of me."

She reached into her purse and shoved a handful of stuff at Nellie. "Look at all this garbage!" she shrilled.

Nellie looked down. There was an old pair of black-framed glasses, a certificate for a free eye exam, and a note that said, "How many fingers am I holding up?"

Nellie pushed it away with her arm. She stood up, grabbing her lunch bag. "Hey, maybe if you'd been helping us out, none of this would've happened. If you're such a hot babysitter, how come all you did was sit around and read *The Poky Little Puppy*? We all know you need to work on your reading skills, but—"

Peggy pulled Nellie back just as Suzi lunged at her. "Nellie, come on."

Hoots of laughter came from the other tables. "Fight, fight, fight!" some boys chanted.

Mr. Miller, the world cultures teacher, and school wrestling coach marched toward them. He had a napkin tucked into his collar to protect his tie from spaghetti sauce.

"Ladies, what seems to be the problem?"

Nellie looked down. Why was it so hard just to turn the other cheek?

Suzi had pulled herself together. She looked, wet-eyed, at Mr. Miller. "I'm sorry, sir. She insulted me."

Nellie opened and closed her mouth. "She started it," Peggy said, glaring at Suzi.

"May I suggest you all apologize? Then return—quietly—to your homerooms and wait for class to resume. If we have another incident, there will be a half-day in-school suspension. Understand?"

Nellie nodded, raising her eyes only as high as the spot of tomato sauce that had just missed Mr. Miller's napkin and landed on his shirt. "Yes, sir."

"I don't know what this world's coming to," Mr. Miller said. "Girls used to be more feminine. You didn't see stuff in the news like what we're hearing about you three—and fights in the cafe-teria!"

He laughed. "But, hey! Maybe we can use you on the wrestling squad, huh?"

As he walked away, Nellie muttered under her breath. "Wait till he hears they gave women the vote."

She turned to Suzi. "Sorry," she mumbled, the word sticking like peanut butter.

Suzi made a snooty noise and stalked away. Peggy looked around for Mr. Miller, then stuck her tongue out at Suzi's back. "I say we make *her* pay for the baby's college."

7

At the Foster Home

The news report of the custody hearing said "Baby Jane Doe" would remain with her foster family while the police continued to investigate. It didn't mention Nellie and Peggy. Afterward the anchorwoman did a segment on emergency foster care that featured the baby's foster mother, a grandmotherly woman who'd once taken in three small boys in the middle of the night.

"It takes a special person," the reporter said, "to take in a child without warning, to love him and care for him and then let him go."

"Why do they have to let them go?" Nellie asked. "Can't the foster parents just adopt the baby?"

"Sometimes," Dad said. "But not often. Usually they try to get the original parents ready to take responsibility. Or assign the child to a family that's been waiting to adopt—like we were when Danny came."

At the sound of his name, Danny pumped his arms and released a stream of drool onto Dad's pantleg. The baby stuffed a fist into his own very expandable mouth and gnawed. Apparently there was a noisy round of teething coming up again tonight.

Nellie wondered how Danny's spit kept flowing like that. He was a natural wonder, like Niagara Falls—on a small scale, of course—and really deserved to be lit up with colored lights at night.

Mom stuck her head in the living room door. "You want to hear a great coincidence? Remember Millie? We used to teach together. Anyway, she does infant foster care now. And guess what?"

Nellie took her eyes away from her drooling brother. "Was that your friend on TV? Does she have Baby Jane?" Nellie asked, focusing.

"Well, no," Mom said. "But she knows the foster mom. They started out doing this at the same time. And Beth—that's her friend—said the baby's doing fine. And she's healthy, except for that leg."

Nellie leaned forward. "Mom, do you think I'd be allowed to visit?"

Mom looked puzzled. "I don't see why you wouldn't, but why?"

"Well. . . ." Mom and Dad had already told Nellie she wouldn't be legally responsible for Janie, but how could they be sure? The foster mother probably would know all that stuff, though. And maybe, Nellie thought hopefully, she could pick up a clue as to where the baby had come from.

Dad was talking, absently wiping drool off himself. "You did your job the best you could when you were babysitting. Now it's up to the police and the foster parents and Children and Youth Services to do their job." He frowned. "And the baby's parents, most of all."

"I know that," Nellie said. Her parents seemed to think she was worrying about Janie. They didn't understand that sometimes a person was just plain curious—especially when she got mixed up with the police and the TV and newspapers. Sometimes, like Lady with the school bus, Nellie couldn't help looking for some excitement. "I just want to say 'hi.' "

Finally Mom agreed. First Mom made a couple calls to make sure it was okay and found out it was. She had errands in Begg City, and she'd wait and do them tomorrow after school. She'd pick Nellie up and drop her off for fifteen minutes—no more.

Begg City was only two miles from home. The road beyond Nellie's house was so bad, though, they always drove the long way through Chestnut Grove. In nice weather, they could bike it. This time of year, it was a ten-minute drive.

Although Begg City was the county seat, Nellie had a feeling Paula's friends wouldn't be any more impressed with it than they were with Chestnut Grove. You could walk all over town and not see anything more thrilling than a pick-up truck fitted with big wheels and chaser lights around the license plate.

Mom pulled along the curb beside a big, red brick house. It had a long, white, railed porch wrapped around two sides. A cluster of cornhusk dolls dressed as Pilgrims hung on the door.

"Don't bother Mrs. Carnahan. She was sweet to say you could stop, but she's caring for two babies now, and her hands are certainly full."

Danny snoozed in his car seat beside Mom, his chin resting on a big, wet patch on the front of his jacket. "We'll be up at the pharmacy, so meet us there, okay?"

Nellie nodded. "Fifteen minutes—promise."

Mom pulled noisily away. Since she was home during the day, they'd needed to buy a second car. At first Nellie had been hopeful. She'd thought anything would be better than their rolling crate of worn-out parts.

Then she saw this thing—the color Dad's face turned when they were stuck in a boat during a storm on Lake Chippewa. Except with rust spots. And it was small enough for Danny to drive around the yard, if they put in some pedals. And come to think of it, that probably wouldn't change the horsepower all that much.

Nellie rang the doorbell, then stuck her cold hand into a jacket pocket. The kindly-looking woman with fading red hair whom Nellie had seen on TV opened the door.

"Nellie Locke?" Mrs. Carnahan smiled. "Come right in."

She led Nellie down a short, high-ceilinged hall draped in shadows. "We're back here in the kitchen."

They walked into a room with old-fashioned canisters that matched worn-looking wallpaper covered with orange and yellow morning glories. A dark-skinned boy with angel's cheeks was banging his spoon on the high chair tray. A chunky woman bending over a half-size playpen jerked around and smiled.

"Oh, hi! I was just admiring the little girl."

Nellie concentrated on not staring. She'd never seen a beehive hairdo on a real person—only in old pictures. But that tall cone of teased-up orange hair really should have had bees buzzing in and out of it, covered with pollen. Nellie had never seen a paint job like the woman had on her face, either.

"Yes, Janie's a dear, isn't she, Lavar?"

The little boy grinned and swung at Mrs. Carnahan's face.

"Now, as I was saying, Miss," went on Mrs. Carnahan, "I really don't think I'm interested in ordering anything today."

The beehive lady's face sagged a little. "Oh, honey, are you sure?" She reached into a case on the table. "This Baja Beige would just warm your skin tone right up."

She was already unscrewing the top. Mrs. Carnahan waved a hand. "No, dear, I really don't think so."

Beehive stuck the Baja Beige back in her case.

55

"Blusher, then. Sonora Sunset."

Beehive had a regular sunset blazing across her own cheekbones, shaded from apple red to a dusky burgundy. Her eyes were so furred with false lashes it must have been hard to see out. Black eyeliner lay like a strip of tar around the lashes. Above that drooped a crescent of glittery purple shadow. Nellie guessed Beehive wanted to display all her products at once.

"No," Mrs. Carnahan said firmly. "I'm sorry, but—"

"Baby lotion?" Beehive tweaked Lavar's cheek, making him frown and drop his spoon. She held up a fat squeeze-bottle of Butter Buns.

"Smell this!" she commanded, sticking it under Nellie's nose. "It's from our Village Bakeshop collection. We also have Coconut Cream, if you prefer."

"No," Mrs. Carnahan repeated. "Nothing today."

Or tomorrow or next week or next year, Nellie thought.

Beehive took her time repacking. She was smiling down at Janie, who lay on her back, gumming on a chew toy. "Maybe another day, huh?"

Mrs. Carnahan shrugged a little—probably the safest answer. Beehive shuffled out past her, the ankles of her pantyhose lying in wrinkled folds above bright turquoise three-inch heels.

"Excuse me," Mrs. Carnahan told Nellie. "I'll be right back."

Nellie picked up Lavar's spoon and handed it to him. Then she walked over and looked down at Janie.

The baby smiled, kicking her good leg. "Hi, Janie. Remember me?"

Mrs. Carnahan came back in. "I'm sorry. I told her I wasn't interested, but she just insisted on showing me. She said she was a widow, and I guess I felt a little sorry for her."

"That's all right," Nellie said. She looked down again at the happy baby. "I can't stay long, anyway. I just wanted to see how she's doing."

"Fine," Mrs. Carnahan said, spreading a handful of Cheerios on Lavar's tray. "She adjusted to us right away."

"How could anyone hurt their own little baby?" Nellie held her fingers out for Janie to grab.

Mrs. Carnahan reached down and lifted the baby. "I don't think most people mean to do it," she said. "The stress just makes them snap. Imagine being a young single mother—maybe only a teenager—and never getting a break."

Nellie shuddered. There had been rumors about one of the seniors at school last spring. Was this how things had turned out for her?

Mrs. Carnahan turned Janie outward, to look around while she got the baby's bottle. "Babies aren't always sweet and quiet, you know."

Nellie made a snorting noise. "Yeah, I found that out."

"I think a lot of parents just need some support to help them handle things," Mrs. Carnahan said.

"Like Peggy and I needed in that nursery," Nellie said, shifting to her other foot. "Uh, Mrs. Carnahan? There's no way *we* could be held responsible for her, is there?"

Mrs. Carnahan shook her head. "Of course not!" She gave Nellie a wry smile. "I hope all this hasn't frightened you off small children forever."

Maybe not forever, Nellie thought, but she'd certainly had enough to last her for the next fifteen years.

8

Dooley,
Dog with a Past

"We won't stay long," Nellie promised Peggy. "I just want to see Aunt Paula's dog."

"Well, the movie starts at 2:15, so if you want popcorn, we have to leave by quarter till."

Mom pulled into a spot along the curb in front of the house. Danny arched his body against the seat harness, making squawky noises.

Nellie felt herself tense against the sound. She'd listened to it all night long, on and off.

"Here." She shoved a teething ring into his hand and he gave it an angry back flip into Peggy's forehead.

"Ow!"

"Mom, when's he going to stop?" Nellie asked.

Mom unsnapped the harness and lifted him out. Her lips looked tight.

"I don't know, Nellie. I gave him something for the fever when we left the house. It ought to work on the sore gums, too. He *is* cutting two teeth at once."

"I'm sorry," Nellie whispered to Peggy, who was rubbing the red bullseye on her forehead.

"It's okay," Peggy mumbled as they trailed Mom up the sidewalk. "How do you stand it?"

"He's usually sweet," Nellie said, rising to defend the family honor. "It's just that his gums hurt."

"That 'nyeh-nyeh' noise all the time would drive me crazy." Peggy's forehead gleamed like a stop light. "I almost wish he'd come out with it—just scream instead of warming up for hours."

"Peggy! You've only been listening to him for ten minutes."

Peggy made a face.

"Hi!" Aunt Paula grabbed Danny as soon as the door opened. "Come on in."

Peggy sneezed.

"God bless you."

She sneezed again.

"You getting a cold?" Nellie asked.

Peggy, shaking her head, blew her nose. "Nuh-uh. I think it's my allergies."

Nellie looked around Aunt Paula's spotless living room. "Not a mold spore in sight."

"My allergist says people change. I think I—" She sneezed again.

"God bless you."

"I think I'm getting allergic to dogs, too."

"Where is your dog, Aunt Paula?"

"Probably hiding." Paula looked around. "He's a little shy yet. Dooley!"

A wet nose appeared around the corner, then a brown eye surrounded by tufts of white hair. Nellie walked over, holding out one hand for him to sniff.

The dog crept toward her, but stopped three feet away. He stretched his neck out.

"Here, Dooley. Nice boy," Nellie said.

Lady's scent brought him closer. Dooley was nearly as big as Mom's new used car. If he ever found his courage, he ought to be a good watchdog.

"What is he?" Peggy asked. She stared at Dooley's huge head, the shaggy fur in patches of black, white, and gray, the big feet with tufts between the toes like a Dr. Seuss creation.

"Just a dog," said Paula, shifting Danny to her other hip. "Some big breeds in there, I guess. Newfoundland or English sheepdog. Maybe St. Bernard. Standard poodle?"

Nellie squinted at the curling plume of tail, now slowly wagging. "Could be some Afghan hound."

Peggy sneezed again and backed away. "He's nice," she said, sounding stuffy.

Nellie sat on the floor and patted him. "Where did you get him, Aunt Paula?"

"Over at the shelter. They found him tied to the door the other day."

Abandoned like Baby Jane. Nellie hugged him.

Dooley sneezed and Nellie laughed. "Hey, he's allergic to us, too."

"The vet thinks he's a young dog," said Paula. "But the nice thing is, he's already housebroken. No puppies for the working girl."

Mom sat down on the couch and Paula sank down next to her, bouncing Danny on her knee. "Don't you wonder where he's been?" Mom said.

Paula grinned. "If only he could talk."

Dooley turned from Nellie and plodded toward the sofa. Paula reached out one hand to pet him. "Yes, Dooley, you're a dog with a past."

Dooley sniffed, poking at the baby with his big, cold nose. Danny flailed his arm.

"Nellie," Paula said, moving Danny away from Dooley's inquiring nose. "There are dog biscuits on the kitchen counter. Why don't you call him in there for a treat? Danny doesn't like being nosed."

Peggy, rubbing at her own nose like she was trying to erase it, headed for the kitchen too. "Can we go soon?" she whispered.

"Yeah, pretty soon," Nellie promised, digging into the box for a nice, big, unbroken biscuit. "Here, Dooley!"

At the sound of the box, Dooley lumbered toward the kitchen. It was probably a pretty energetic pace for a clumsy young dog his size. When he hit the kitchen tiles, his toenails clicked and skidded.

He jumped up on his hind legs, making Aunt Paula's coffeemaker and mug tree rattle. "Dooley, get down!"

Surprisingly, he did, still wiggling and wagging all over. He was like a baby hippo with fur.

"Good dog," Nellie said, tossing the biscuit. "Somebody must have trained him. Lady would never obey like that."

Peggy sneezed hard enough to loosen her brains. So did Dooley. "God bless you," Nellie said, reclosing the biscuit box.

Dooley pinned his treat to the floor with a massive paw and gnawed at the other end. Saliva puddled beneath his jaws.

"She ought to call him Drooley," Peggy muttered. "Can we wash the dog dander off our hands?"

"The what?"

"The stuff that's making me—" Peggy sneezed again.

"Okay, okay." Nellie ran water. "Here." She shoved soap at Peggy.

"I don't know why it's bothering you," Nellie said. "Lady never seemed to."

Peggy shrugged and sniffed. "I think he's shedding."

She was wiping her hands on the seat of her jeans as they walked back into the living room. "Can we leave, Mom?" Nellie asked.

Mom nodded. "I'm going to drop the girls at the movies and run my errands," she told Aunt Paula. "We'll be back for Danny in a couple hours."

"No problem. Danny and I are going to do the laundry. You need to train these guys early."

Danny sat propped against pillows in a corner of the couch. He began to squawk, sawing at his gum with one fist.

Paula hurried to pick him up. "Boy, you men are all alike."

Nellie turned her head at the scrabble of claws against floor tiles. Dooley slid around the corner.

"Come here, handsome." Paula reached for Danny, who was waving his arms with each angry bellow.

Nellie gasped. "Aunt Paula!"

Dooley skidded to a stop a few feet from the couch, a low rumble coming from the back of his throat as he fixed Paula with a cold eye. The fur at the back of his neck actually seemed to bristle.

Aunt Paula's friend had warned her about getting a bad dog from the shelter. Remembering what he'd said, Nellie felt her heart bang against her chest. Dooley's lip curled, revealing strong jaws and pointed teeth.

Peggy screeched and jumped onto the armchair. "Get away, get away!"

She climbed onto the chair back, the lace doily sliding under her knee. She made a shoving motion with her hand as her eyes darted around, probably in search of a weapon.

Peggy's leap distracted the dog. He turned to her, barking as if he'd treed a squirrel.

Peggy sneezed mightily and had to clutch the chair to keep from falling.

"Dooley!" Mom and Paula both shouted.

He stopped barking and turned to grin, wagging his tail. "Good dog," Mom told him.

Paula reached again for Danny, who was quietly gnawing on the bottom of his shirt. The dog took two steps toward the sofa and stopped again, looking confused.

"It's okay, Dool," Aunt Paula said. "Good boy. I'm not hurting him—see?"

She held Danny on one hip, stretching a hand out to pat the dog's head. Dooley slowly wagged his tail, looking from Paula and Danny to Peggy, who was still perched on the back of the chair. He didn't look dangerous anymore—just anxious and a bit confused.

"He's really protective of the baby," Paula said. "How sweet."

"He's darling," Peggy muttered. "And fast for his size."

9

The Dark-Haired Girl

Nellie liked the last Saturday of each month. That was when Peggy went to the orthodontist to get her braces adjusted. Nellie always met her, and they'd walk around the mall afterward.

The last couple of months, Rick had shown up, too. Nellie suspected he planned it, but she wasn't sure enough of herself to count on it. When she saw him heading toward her seat at Spuds 'n' More, she felt that little lifting sensation.

He grinned. "Hi, Nell. You waiting for Peggy?"

She nodded. "She's getting the wires off today. Maybe." Peggy's doctor had a way of deciding at the last minute to tighten them up and keep them on a little longer.

"I'm going to grab a drink. You want something?"

Although her cup was drained, Nellie shook her head. "I'm just going to chew ice."

While Rick went up to the counter, Nellie crunched, poking at the remaining cubes with her straw. When he returned, she asked, "Did you see the paper?"

He slid into his seat. "Yeah. Don't take it seriously."

"I can't help it." Nellie slumped onto her elbows. Even the aroma rising from Rick's basket of twisty fries didn't rouse her. "Every girl in the county is going to hate me."

Rick twirled a fry in catsup. "I doubt it. Why should they?" He popped the fry into his mouth, then followed it with a whole greasy handful.

"Because," Nellie said, "most of us have one source of income. We babysit. Period.

"How popular is the person going to be who single-handedly brings on a whole rash of letters to the editor saying not to hire teenage babysitters?"

Rick wiped his mouth and fingers. "Come on. They didn't really say that."

"Yes, they did. They said teenage girls are still children themselves, that we're not responsible, that we're all thinking about our boyfriends—" Nellie felt her face go red, but Rick didn't seem to notice.

He said, "Well, really they just mostly said things like, 'My mother never left us with a babysitter and this is what happens today' or, 'Do you really want to leave your precious baby with someone who's too busy talking on the phone to—' "

"Rick," Nellie interrupted. "It's all the same." She grabbed one of his twisty fries and scrunched it into a tight spring. It flopped when she released it.

"Well. . . ." Rick kept trying to help. "You weren't exactly single-handed. Peggy and Suzi were—"

Nellie tossed the dead fry onto the tray. "Oh, that makes a big difference. And anyway, Suzi was the first one in line to holler at me for ruining her babysitting business."

"That stuff in the cafeteria? She didn't mean it. She's just high-strung."

Nellie thought, *She's a blond cheerleader, too. That makes anything she says all right.* But she didn't say it. Instead, she sighed.

"It's been two weeks and the police haven't found a thing."

"We don't know that," Rick said. "Or at least I don't. Just because they're not filling me in doesn't mean anything."

Nellie slapped both hands on the table, leaning forward. "But I have to know. If there's nothing on the news, how can I know if they're even trying?"

"Nellie, you know they're trying." Rick used the voice you use to reason with a grouchy toddler.

She sank against the seat back. "I know, I know. I guess I just want to be doing something myself. We were right there when it happened, and now they won't tell us anything. When we had that trouble in the graveyard, at least we could do our own investigation."

Rick gave up. "Have some fries. You'll feel better."

When Peggy arrived, she was smiling an odd, stiff grin. "They're gone," she said, running her tongue around. "It's like my teeth are going to pop out."

"Hey, great," Nellie said. "Congratulations."

"Fries?" Rick offered the basket, which at this point only contained three fries and a bunch of salt.

Peggy shook her head. "My mouth doesn't feel right."

"You want to walk around then?" Nellie asked.

"Sure."

"Rick?"

He didn't answer. His eyes were fixed on a girl with a long, dark ponytail. She was standing, back turned, looking into the window of the T-shirt shop.

"Rick!" Nellie couldn't keep that sharp note out of her voice. The sight of him eyeing some long-legged girl in jeans made her heart lurch.

He half-rose from his seat, ignoring Nellie, his eyes focused on the other girl. When the girl turned to cross to the other side, Nellie caught her profile. She was maybe a year older than Nellie—or maybe the makeup just made her look that way.

"Come on!" Rick's whisper was urgent. He

grabbed his fleece-lined jean jacket off the chair back.

A hip-high wall separated Spuds 'n' More seating from the mall walkers. Rick sprinted the opposite direction from the dark-haired girl, so he could get around the barrier.

Peggy just stared after him, but Nellie suddenly realized this was something other than infatuation. He had recognized that girl.

Nellie pushed back from the table, making it screech and tilt. She grabbed and steadied it, then caught Peggy's arm.

"Come on," she repeated, dodging around a mother carrying a loaded tray and dragging a double stroller.

"Hey, watch it!" Peggy complained, jerking her arm free. "She sloshed some of her drink when you went around her and I almost fell in it."

"No, she didn't," Nellie said, following Rick's jean jacket as he darted through the crowd ahead. "The floor was already wet."

Rick momentarily vanished into a thicket of senior citizens. "I lost him!" she wailed, eyes searching for a familiar thatch of dark hair among the snowcaps.

"Over there!" Peggy called. "By the escalator."

Nellie got to the crowd, who were all wearing bus tour tags. "Excuse me," she sputtered. "Excuse me."

People moved out of her way, but slowly. Nellie tried not to shove. It was hard not to just put her head down and burrow through.

"Excuse me," Peggy said behind her. "I'm sorry. Nellie, wait."

Nellie moaned, searching for Rick with her eyes. That looked like him over by the north entrance.

She looked back at Peggy, who was trying to untangle the sleeve button of her jacket from an old lady's mesh shopping bag. Between Peggy and the woman, it looked to Nellie like they were just twisting it in deeper.

Nellie glanced back to where she'd last seen Rick. He must have gone out into the parking lot.

Peggy still struggled in the net like the catch of the day. "Excuse me," she kept saying. "I'm sorry."

"I'll be back," Nellie promised. Then she added, "Stay there," just in case Peggy and the woman decided to hobble after her.

Hitting a clear space, Nellie ran. Had Rick seen the dark-haired girl at the Community Church that day? Nellie couldn't remember ever seeing her, but maybe—a guy would remember a pretty girl better than she would.

There was no sign of Rick in the mass of faces in the wide corridor near the entrance. Nellie scanned left and right as she slowed to a trot, panting.

Finally, a stab of pain in her side made her stop. She half-doubled, pressing her hands against the hurt, and backed up to the wall.

Some people passing by gave her a look. She straightened up as much as she could to show

71

them she was all right.

Peggy trotted up. "Where's Rick?"

"I don't know. Maybe he went out." Nellie walked that way, rubbing at her side.

"I told you to wait," she added, irritated.

"I couldn't. That lady wanted me to meet her grandson—Butchie."

Nellie pushed against the heavy glass door. "Well, I did notice you'd gotten real 'attached' to her."

"Not enough to go out with Butchie."

"Maybe he's cute," Nellie said, searching the lot for Rick.

"If he was cute he wouldn't have to send his granny out with a net to find his dates."

Nellie giggled. Then she saw Rick. He was plodding toward them from across the lot, still looking to both sides as he came.

She broke into a trot again, but he waved her down, pointing to the stretch of curb in front of the entrance. When they all met there, Rick plopped down. The girls sat beside him.

Nellie looked at his face. He was still breathing hard, still looking all around the parking lot.

"Who was she?" Nellie asked.

"I don't know. If I hadn't lost her, maybe we could find out." He threw a piece of gravel at the base of a lamp pole.

Rick turned to Nellie, dark eyes full of frustration. "She was there at the church last week—and acting strange."

10

Search for the Girl

Nellie stared at Rick. "All this time you didn't say one word about a girl."

He gave her a look. "We were trying to remember people with babies, not teenagers. But when I saw her, I knew right away she'd been there."

"Tell us everything you can remember," Peggy told him.

He got to his feet. "Okay. But inside. It's too cold out here."

They returned to the doors, Rick taking one last long look around the parking lot.

"You sure she went outside?" Nellie asked.

He shrugged, making a face. "I thought so. But no—not a hundred percent."

"Then let's walk up and down and check the shops," she suggested.

"And we can look in the rest rooms," Peggy added.

"All right."

As they walked along, Nellie kept an ear on Rick and her eyes searching inside the stores for a dark-haired girl. It got pretty confusing.

"Rick! Excuse me—look. Is that her?"

"No. Her ponytail came to here. And it wasn't braided.

"Anyway," Rick continued. "It was late—near the end of the meeting. I see this girl leaving the church—coming out the side door near the parking lot.

"It was dark along there, so I didn't get a great look. First I didn't think much, except maybe that the meeting was over."

Peggy grabbed his arm and pointed.

He shook his head. "She was wearing jeans. And a red jacket."

"Can we walk to the back?" Nellie asked, pulling him toward Domenica's. "I want to look around the dressing rooms."

"Okay. Anyway, she kind of scuffled along in the shadows and headed for the sidewalk out front. I didn't pay a lot of attention, because a couple people had to leave early, and they were blocked in.

"But when I saw her just now, I remembered. She had a ski tag or something dangling off her pocket and a tear in the left shoulder. And I started to think—there were only a few teenagers there that night. *Us*. And we were all working."

"So who was she?" Peggy concluded, peering around a rack jammed with parkas.

"This is hopeless." Nellie sighed. "Even if she's

still inside, the mall's too big. She could be up-stairs. She could be in one of the department stores. She could be walking fifty feet in front of us."

"I know," Rick said. "But we may as well look."

Looking for a particular teenager at the mall on a Saturday afternoon was like trying to iden-tify one special blade of grass. By the time they'd walked from one end of the building to the other, then back again on the upper level, Nellie was rubbing the ache between her eyes.

"I've got to go," Rick said, checking his watch. "I'm meeting Mom back down at the north en-trance."

"My mom will be coming for us, too," Peggy said. "We'll walk down with you."

Nellie sagged, one hand on the rail, and let the escalator carry her. "Are you going to call the po-lice?"

She watched the back of Rick's head as he nodded. "I thought I'd do that as soon as I get home."

"And I'll call the Community Church," Nellie said, "and ask if anybody who looks like that girl is a member over there."

"It's a pretty big church." Peggy's gloomy voice came from behind her. "They've probably got ten kids who look like her."

"So we'll check 'em out," Nellie said.

Peggy caught her arm as they stepped off the escalator. "She's like our age, Nell. Do you think she could actually be Baby Jane's—" She stopped, as if the idea was too mind-boggling.

"Mother?" Nellie said. She knew it happened, but like Peggy, she just couldn't imagine what it would be like. Mothers were—mothers. Girls like she and Peggy were big sisters or babysitters—and some people thought they weren't even responsible enough for that.

What would it be like to know you were the only mom some poor baby had? Nellie shuddered. "That could explain why the baby was abandoned," she admitted. "I can see where being fourteen and having to take care of a baby could make you want to run away."

Rick turned, his eyes darker than usual. "Who says she was running away? Maybe she just decided the baby would be better off."

Nellie's face burned as she found herself following Rick, staring at his back. His own adoption was never any big deal, so she always tended to forget about it. "I didn't mean it like that."

She touched his shoulder. "I just meant—I can see where she might have thought leaving the baby was best. For everybody."

Lowering her voice, she added, "It may have been her way of trying to take care of the baby." She wasn't just talking about Baby Jane's mother.

Rick gave her a sideways glance. His face had relaxed a little. "I know." He took her hand. "It's just I think about her a lot lately—my birth mom. She was fifteen. Only a year older than I am. In a way, I really do understand, but in another way, I think, hey, how could she just let me go?"

Nellie glanced over her shoulder at Peggy, who was hanging back, giving them space. "God put you with your mom and dad, remember? Whatever happened." Nellie squeezed his fingers. "And he's taking care of her, too."

Rick returned the squeeze. "Thanks, Nellie."

She swallowed. "Hey, I'm only saying what you told me about Danny, which I thought was very smart at the time."

"It's a good thing God's there to straighten things out," Rick said. "Because people can sure mess them up."

"No kidding," Nellie agreed, drooping a little now that the excitement of the chase was over. Where had she gone, that girl with dark hair like Baby Jane? Would it be kinder—for everybody—just to let her disappear?

11

Where Did You Come From?

Later in the day, Nellie turned her back on an untouched stack of homework. It sat on the ledge between the kitchen and sunporch. The sunporch, really an old-fashioned, windowed family room, ran the length of the house.

Hunched knees-up in a corner of the hard old sofa, she pressed the phone receiver close to her ear. Mom and Aunt Paula were chattering so loudly in the kitchen, it was hard to hear anything else. Half the time the two of them talked at once, not even waiting for the other to answer.

"I'm sorry," Nellie said. "I didn't hear that."

Staring hard out the windows, she listened again. There had been a killing frost Friday night, and everything outside drooped under a powder dusting of early snow.

"I said," Reverend Weimer said, raising his voice, "I can't think of anybody who really fits that description. We can run through our pictorial directory and see what we come up with, but I'm afraid I can't be too encouraging."

Thanking him, Nellie hung up, knocking her books onto the kitchen floor in the process. The paper avalanche got Lady and Dooley's attention. Both clicked over to stick clammy noses into her hands and face as she hung over the ledge, scooping up her stuff.

Unfortunately, Mom noticed, too. "Nellie, have you finished your work yet?"

"Not quite," Nellie admitted breathlessly, lungs flattened by the shelf and all the blood rushing to the tips of her dangling hair.

"It's getting late, and Peggy's coming right after dinner. If you'd at least get started after school on Friday—"

"I know, I know," Nellie gasped, straightening up. She slammed everything back, more or less in place. "But I just want to relax Friday night. If you'd let me do it Sunday like everybody else, I'd be rested up."

"Nellie, we've discussed this. Sundays are for church and family time. You just need to get yourself organized."

Sliding back into her seat, Nellie tried to turn her mind from the puzzle of Baby Jane back to her history assignment, where it belonged. School could be a mystery, but not the kind she was interested in at the moment. Her thoughts ran in all directions, like sheep, while she tried to herd them together.

Mrs. Wagner had warned her this week about

her work. Something about "people who don't learn the lessons of history are doomed to repeat it." Wagner had chuckled about that, but Nellie failed to see the humor. She could never remember dates, and she couldn't bear another term of this.

All the same, Nellie's mind kept wandering to Rick and his call to the police. It was too soon to call him, but still she wondered.

It was dark by the time she'd finished her homework. The kitchen door slammed. "Barn-work's done!" Dad called. The house smelled of tomato sauce, barn clothes, wet dog, and baby powder.

Nellie focused on the tomato sauce. Her stomach rumbled.

She walked into the kitchen with the feeling she was emerging from hibernation. Dad was washing at the sink.

Nellie stretched. "Where is everybody?" Dad asked over his shoulder.

TV sounds came from the living room. Nellie jerked a thumb. "In there, I guess."

She opened the oven door on the cookstove and sniffed. Eggplant parmesan—one of Mom's better efforts. At least, it was one of the few that didn't involve soybeans, seaweed, or rice.

Nellie turned around to see Dad rooting through the fridge with an empty glass in one hand. She wrinkled her nose at his essence-of-barn aroma.

He came up with the plastic jug of cider.

"Homework done?"

"Of course." She wasn't some eight-year-old deadbeat, for crying out loud. "You want to change while I fix that?" Nellie asked, ever-hopeful. She didn't ever expect her family to dress up for dinner, but she did think Dad could at least change the barn clothes.

"No thanks." He smiled, pouring. "I've got it."

Dad stuck the cider back in the fridge. "Think I'll go see my boy."

It still felt strange, hearing Dad call Danny that. For thirteen years, Nellie had been Dad's only kid. They'd always been really close. But Dad would never call her "my boy." Maybe it hurt a little that Danny could fill a place in Dad's life which Nellie never could.

She followed Dad across the darkened hall into the living room. One lamp burned on the table and images jumped across the TV screen. The sound was turned soft. It was an old episode of *The Rockford Files*.

Danny slept against Mom's shoulder, Paula sitting beside her on the couch. The dogs slept at their feet, Lady with her chin on Mom's shoe.

Nellie and Dad walked in just as an argument erupted on the screen. The actors, James Garner and Rita Moreno, yelled at each other, startling Dooley out of his dog dreams.

His head popped up in a look of confusion.

"It's okay, Dool," Aunt Paula said, reaching to pat him as he scrambled to his feet.

The TV argument heated up. Nellie had seen

81

this episode a hundred times. It was funny stuff.

Dooley's eyes restlessly searched the room. He paced—looking, sniffing.

James Garner hollered something and Rita Moreno yelled back. Dooley rumbled in his throat and pushed past Dad into the hall.

"What on earth?" Mom glanced from the doorway to Paula.

Nellie heard the click of Dooley's toenails on the kitchen floor. This way. That way.

He whined and yipped.

Paula got up. "Maybe he needs to go out."

But as she walked toward the doorway, Dooley came back in. *Electrified*, Nellie thought. That was the word for how he was acting. Even the ruff at the back of his neck stood up like he'd had a shock.

Lady sat up, looking interested but puzzled. Paula reached for Dooley again. He shot away from her hand, paying her no attention, continuing his search.

James Garner cruised down the coast road now. Rita Moreno was gone.

"Dooley," Aunt Paula said, sitting on the floor.

For the first time, he seemed to notice her. He came over, head and tail low. His ears drooped.

Aunt Paula hugged and petted him. "Poor old Dool. Did you have a bad dream?"

"Guess he's not a James Garner fan," Dad said.

Paula shook her head. "I think it was that argument on TV. He always seems to get worked up when anybody raises his voice."

Nellie sat down beside them. She reached a cautious hand toward Dooley's furry shoulder.

Dooley looked at her. His brown eyes were deep, full of things he couldn't tell her about. He looked as though he'd like to tell her—as if he were begging her to try to understand.

She shook her head. It was crazy to try to read a dog's mind. It was probably only full of dog biscuits, garbage cans and squirrels, anyway.

"Poor Dool," Aunt Paula repeated, stroking his fur. "Where did you come from? What happened to make you like this?"

12

Baby Burnout

Danny's look, as Nellie set him back in his seat, was accusing. He screamed again, his face gleaming with tears. She could see all the way past red gums down to his tonsils.

The phone rang again. "Sorry," Nellie told him. "I'll be right back."

Peggy had arrived with her backpack full of overnight stuff just as Nellie's folks left to take Aunt Paula and Dooley home. She was watching her popcorn-in-progress like a technician at some nuclear power plant. She gave Nellie an apologetic smile.

"Hello?" Nellie plugged her other ear with a finger.

"Nellie, it's Rick. Did you have any luck with Reverend Weimer?"

"No!" she shouted over screams. "He said he'd call if he found anyone who matched our description, but he didn't expect much."

"I told the police. They had someone make a sketch. They'll check at the other churches and maybe run it on the news."

Nellie leaned against the wall, trying not to listen to Danny. Detective work beat babysitting any day. "Maybe we can track her down ourselves."

"How?"

The popping had stopped and Peggy was melting butter. Nellie covered the receiver, nodding toward Danny. "Hey, get him—will you?"

Peggy pushed the pan of butter to the cool side of the stove, eyeing Danny uneasily.

"Well, maybe we can check the schools and the burger places and hangouts Monday afternoon."

Rick sighed. "The police will already be doing that. And how do we get to Begg City? It's not bike weather."

"Well, maybe one of our parents would take us."

"Not unless we were going to the library or something. And we don't even know where the hangouts are over there."

"Well, Davey Dee's, probably, for one. We can figure that out," Nellie insisted, trying to convince herself as well as Rick. "We know some kids over there.

"Excuse me. Peggy, try putting him in his jumping thing or the swing."

Peggy shifted Danny to her other hip, holding him as far as she could from her ear, and headed for the living room. Lady, following, looked back and yipped at Nellie.

Nellie pressed her finger harder against her ear. "Look. I know we can do better than the police. We think like teenagers; they don't."

"Maybe. But that's not all there is to it."

"Such as?"

"Well, Baby Jane's about Danny's age. Even if that girl's the baby's mother, there's no way she could keep it a secret for four or five months."

Nellie thought about it.

"There's no way you can hide a kid in your room for five months. If she's really the mother, there are grownups who know about it, too."

"So let the police look for them," Nellie agreed. "But I bet I can find that girl myself."

She heard another sigh. "And what'll you do when you find her?" Rick wanted to know.

"Look," she told him. "I've got to go. Danny's really out of control. I'll talk to you after church tomorrow." Maybe by then, she'd have a clue about what came next if she actually found Baby Jane's mother.

Danny was slumped as low in the swing as his kicking and arching could get him. At the sight of Nellie, he pumped his arms and yelled harder.

Peggy stopped singing "Itsy Bitsy Spider." She still had a couple yellowish drops of formula clinging to her face. "He threw his bottle," Peggy told her, sounding like a kindergarten tattletale.

"Where is it?" Nellie asked. Then she noticed Lady. The dog had half-crammed herself under the couch to lick the floor. "Never mind. I found it."

"I'll get a fresh one," Peggy offered, eagerly escaping to the kitchen.

Nellie stuck her arm under the sofa. Lady, startled, snapped.

"Lady!" Nellie stared as the dog slunk into the corner by the TV. "What's gotten into you?"

Lady just looked guilty, her normally perky ears drooping. Nellie pulled the bottle out. It was covered with dust bunnies.

She set it on the windowsill and picked up Danny. "Come on, big guy. Let's go for a walk."

One thing she'd learned about Danny's moods was it paid to keep him moving. His stroller was in the closet under the stairs. She was pulling it out when Peggy returned.

"Here." Peggy handed her a fresh bottle. "I'll get it."

She gave a mighty tug and the stroller came out—together with a stack of boxes it had apparently been supporting. The girls jumped out of the way.

"Oh, man!" Peggy shook her head, kicking aside a broken radio. "What do you want with the stroller, anyway?"

"I'm going to walk Danny around the downstairs until he falls asleep." Nellie looked down at her brother, who was staring back with bottomless black eyes. At least the crash had seemed to stop his crying.

She settled him into his seat and gave him his

bottle. "Can you—?"

Peggy started shoving things in boxes. "All right, all right. Just get him to sleep so I can get back to my popcorn."

Nellie pushed the stroller out into the kitchen. Her right foot skidded out from under her as she stepped onto the tiles.

She landed hard. It wasn't funny like when Oliver Hardy or Chevy Chase did it.

Her tailbone felt kind of numb, but sharp pain radiated into her legs. She tried to bend herself enough to stand up, but everything had stiffened. With all the grace of a newborn elephant, Nellie lurched to her feet, wincing at muscles that screamed, "Stop!"

"Are you okay?" Peggy grabbed her arm. "What happened?"

Nellie leaned against her friend, wiping tears with a sweatshirt sleeve. She was still breathing hard, trying not to sob. She shook her head.

"Oh, yuck." Peggy looked at the floor. "What's that?"

Nellie reached around and felt the big, wet spot on the seat of her jeans. "That's what I slipped in."

Suspicious, she sniffed at her fingers. "Lady!"

The dog slunk as far as the corner and looked around at Nellie. Lady's face sagged with apology.

The pain made Nellie want to yell. "*Bad* dog! Why did you wet the floor? You know better than that."

Lady disappeared onto the sunporch. Nellie followed.

"Come here, you!" She grabbed Lady's collar. "Out. You go out for a while."

Tugging open the door, she pushed the dog out. Lady seemed eager to go, unsure what Nellie might do. Nellie slammed the door so the glass rattled.

Peggy held up two handsful of newspapers. "These are from the stack in the corner. Is it okay to use them to soak up the puddle?"

Nellie nodded. Suddenly she just wanted to lie across her bed and cry.

She limped over to check on Danny. Asleep. His dark lashes fanned across cheeks glowing from within like warm honey. He could have been a little angel, sleeping with wings tucked under him.

"Fresh from the hand of God," Grandma Locke always said about babies. Nellie saw what she meant.

Later, when Danny was in bed, she and Peggy ate the popcorn. "I don't know, Peg. Taking care of a baby can really burn you out."

She threw a kernel to Lady, who'd been forgiven. The dog caught it in flight.

"When did you notice?"

Nellie ignored the sarcasm. "It even got to Lady."

She stretched out her legs, staring at her toes wiggling in red socks. "Maybe if I had a baby—"

Nellie paused and swallowed. "Maybe if I had a baby and had to take care of it all by myself, I could really lose it. My temper, I mean—like I did with Lady."

Peggy looked at her. "What?"

"Well—" Nellie searched for words. "It's like Mrs. Carnahan told me. Maybe Baby Jane's mother just kind of snapped from all the pressure. Maybe she didn't mean to hurt her. So she'd be sorry now, and maybe she thinks Janie's better off without her."

Settling wood popped inside the cookstove. The sap fizzed.

Peggy tossed a handful of popcorn into her mouth and washed it down with cider. Finally she said, "So you're thinking, 'What's so bad with the way things are?' "

Nellie nodded and winced, shifting her weight. Even her eyelashes hurt. "I mean—the baby's okay now. Why's it so important to find the mother? To punish her? Maybe it's better this way."

She looked up at Peggy again. Her friend was frowning. "I don't know," Peggy said. "Do you think that's fair? Don't you think Baby Jane will want to know who her mother is someday?"

Nellie rested her cheek against her fist. They'd find Janie's mother—or the police would. But what then?

13

Nellie Has a Brainstorm

Nellie lay in bed that night, thoughts milling. She listened when Danny cried and Mom got up, creaking across the floor to him. He quieted as soon as he heard her. Then the only sound was Mom's soft voice.

Peggy slept, ears plugged, through the crying and creaking. She never twitched when Lady began chasing rabbits in her sleep.

Nellie heard it all. She also heard an owl call from the trees and a freight train hoot back from the crossing. Drifting close to sleep, but never quite there, she thought about how to track down that dark-haired girl. Then the uncomfortable thought that maybe she should just let it alone pricked at her.

Listening to Mom in the next room, Nellie wondered. If they didn't find Janie's mother, someone else would adopt and love her. Would it be so bad if her first mother just faded away like a freight whistle in the night?

The next afternoon, Peggy went home from church with her parents. Dad and Mom wanted to make a hospital visit with old Mrs. Foster, who'd broken her hip.

So Nellie and Danny were waiting at Aunt Paula's. While Danny slept in his carrier, Paula had constructed real sundaes for their dessert. After shoveling on hot fudge sauce and whipped cream, she topped each one with a maraschino cherry.

Nellie picked hers up by the stem and savored, eyes closed. Mom always said that they weren't real, that you might as well put paint and perfume in your mouth. But Nellie liked them.

Dooley lay on the kitchen rug, chin on his front paws. His eyes went back and forth as Nellie and Aunt Paula ate, just in case something good fell his way. But he wasn't excited, the way Lady got at mealtime. The furrow between his eyes gave him a worried expression.

Nellie moved on to the whipped cream, digging a trench around the rim of the bowl. "Aunt Paula?"

"Mm-hmm."

"Do you think it's wrong to find Baby Jane's mother?"

Paula dabbed her whipped cream mustache with a napkin. She raised her eyebrows. "What do you mean, Nellie?"

Nellie explained. She could talk to Aunt Paula better than she could to a lot of other people. It was kind of like talking to a big sister, but without the fighting.

Paula nodded. For the first time, Nellie noticed a couple of little lines at the corners of her aunt's eyes. They made her look a bit sad. "I see what you mean, Nell."

She leaned back, cradling her coffee mug. For a moment, Nellie thought she wouldn't say more.

Aunt Paula took a sip of coffee. She made a face, setting it down. "Cold already. Nell, I guess I think the truth is almost always best. There are times we don't need to dig out everything just because it happens to be true—times when the truth can be hurtful. But if we always remember the love, I don't think we'll go too far wrong in that direction."

Nellie creased her brow like Dooley. "Love?"

"The Bible says we should speak the truth in love. If we try to deal with people lovingly—" She shrugged. "We should come out all right."

Nellie licked fudge sauce from her spoon. "But what *is* the loving thing to do here?"

Paula smiled and patted her hand. "That's a question for God. But you might think about when Janie's older and she wonders who left her here, and why."

The conversation stopped right there as Danny, waking in a strange place, squawked in alarm. Nellie's thoughts vanished like cockroaches under a board.

"Here you go, cookie." Aunt Paula jumped up and reached for the baby. "Come see what—"

Her sentence broke in half as Dooley, suddenly alert, lunged at her hands. "Ow! Dooley, no!"

As soon as Paula yelled, the dog cringed aside, ducking his head. Nellie was on her feet, brandishing the ice-cream scoop. Sticky vanilla rivulets trickled down her arm.

"It's okay, Nellie. Put your weapon down."

Aunt Paula was holding Danny and looking down at her left wrist. She wiped it against her skirt. "Just a little dog drool," she explained.

Nellie could see a red mark—what looked like a tiny nick, a greenish bruise already forming around it. "He *bit* you."

Paula sat back down with Danny on her lap. "He snapped all right." She glanced at Dooley, who sat hunch-shouldered in the too-small space by the refrigerator. His worry lines had deepened, and he looked uncertain, like someone wondering if an apology might not be in order.

"What's wrong, Dooley?" Paula crooned to him the way she did to the baby. "I won't hurt him. It's all right."

She reached a hand out. "I know you didn't mean it. I know. Come here now."

Dooley approached, head down. Just as he got to her feet, he rolled onto his back.

"Dogs do that to tell you you're the boss," Aunt Paula said. "He must be scared." She petted him. "It's okay, Dooley. I know you could've really bitten me, but you didn't. You were just warning me not to hurt Danny, weren't you?"

"Babies are sure hard on dogs," Nellie observed.

Paula gave Danny his teething ring. "He does seem to get Dooley worked up," she agreed.

"Lady, too. She's not acting like herself at all lately."

"Well, it is stressful. Even for people. Babies are noisy; they're demanding. And sometimes when people are upset with the baby, they take it out on the dog."

Nellie took a huge spoonful of ice cream and let it melt on her tongue. She felt an idea coming on.

"Aunt Paula?" Nellie leaned forward. "Do you think maybe Dooley's not just stressed out? Maybe something happened to him before you got him."

Paula bent to pick up the teething ring Danny had dropped. She came up frowning. "He does really act peculiar," she admitted.

"And it's not just the baby," Nellie added. "He got all bothered just hearing people argue on TV."

"I guess we'll never know, Nell. It's not like he can tell us his life story."

Nellie abandoned her sundae to get down on the floor and scratch behind Dooley's ears. She winced as she bent over, still sore from her fall. "Is he always droopy like this?"

Paula shook her head. "He's not much more than a puppy—a huge puppy. Usually he's pretty active."

"Maybe he's like this because Danny's here. He acts like he's expecting something awful to happen."

As she said the words, Nellie's thoughts formed into something she could get hold of. She looked up at Paula, eyes wide.

Awkwardly scrambling back into her seat, Nellie found her hands were almost shaking. "Aunt Paula, look at what upsets him: crying babies, anger, loud voices, anybody touching the baby when he's crying." She raised her eyebrows, waiting for Paula to draw the same conclusion she was coming to.

"It makes you wonder," Paula said, gently bouncing the now-smiling Danny. "It sounds like you're describing an abusive household."

Nellie scooped melted ice cream and sauce into her mouth and swallowed. "It does, doesn't it? Look how Lady gets upset just with the crying. How would it be if things were tense all the time—crying, yelling, hitting?"

"A dog might learn to snap," Paula agreed. "With some dogs, it's natural to protect children, anyway. And when they jump in to do that, sometimes the dog gets hurt, too."

"When exactly did you get him, Aunt Paula?"

She frowned in thought. "Early last—no, almost two weeks ago."

"Did they say where he came from?"

"The shelter people didn't know. He was just left tied to the door, and they found him when they came to work."

"When?" Nellie tried to hold down her excitement. She knew her idea might sound crazy, but somehow it felt right.

Paula shrugged. "I don't know. Not long before I got him, but I'm not sure exactly what day. What are you getting at?"

Nellie grabbed her hand. "Don't you see? Both Baby Jane and Dooley dropped in out of nowhere about the same time. We know Baby Jane came from an abusive home. And now it looks like Dooley did, too. Pretty big coincidence, huh?"

14

At the Animal Shelter

Aunt Paula focused a lot faster than Mom and Dad. "Oh, Nellie, that does seem far-fetched. But, hey—this isn't New York City. How many abandoned babies—or dogs—do we get?"

"Take me to the shelter," Nellie begged.

Paula glanced at her wall clock. "Your folks will be here soon. And, anyway, I'm not sure the shelter's open on Sundays."

"They said 2:30. You know that means at least 3:00," Nellie persisted. "It won't take us more than forty-five minutes to get out there and back."

Paula seemed to hesitate. "Please," Nellie urged, pulling out the phone book. "I'll call and check their hours, and we can leave a note on the door for Mom and Dad."

She turned pages with anxious fingers. At last there was something solid she could do, people she could talk to. "Oh, please, Aunt Paula!"

"Well—Go ahead and call, anyway."

Nellie grinned. "Oh, thank you, thank you. I'll do anything for you—wash and wax your car, walk Dooley—hey, I'll even wash and wax Dooley."

Dooley, lying head on paws, raised his eyebrows to deliver a reproachful look. "Just kidding, Dool. Heh, heh."

She pulled the phone closer and flattened the directory out beside it. One finger marking the number, Nellie dialed.

On the fourth ring, just as her heart started to sink, someone picked up. Dogs barked, yipped, and bayed in the background.

"Yes," a lady's voice told her. "We're open till 5:00 this afternoon, and weeknights except Monday until 8:00."

Paula turned in at a low, sprawling building of white concrete block. An assortment of dogs ran, barking, to fling themselves against the wire-fenced runs out front. Even with the windows rolled up, Nellie could hear why the shelter had to sit among the cornfields without a neighbor in earshot.

The car crunched over gravel to a space under a big, winter-bare tree at the edge of the lot. As Aunt Paula unbuckled Danny from his seat, Nellie looked around at all the cars.

"Busy place."

"On weekends, yes."

"Adopt a Friend—Let Us Make You Smile!"

Nellie read the words splashed in red and black paint on the wall by the door. She stepped aside for a young man with a dancing black Labrador mix, then trailed Paula inside.

"Pee-yew!" Nellie said, gagging on the warm gust of urine and disinfectant cleaner.

Paula smiled and winked. "We'll have to wait a minute. May as well look around."

Four people stood around the counter holding puppies and paperwork as they waited their turns. An elderly couple came in the door behind Nellie.

"Can we take a number?" Nellie asked.

Paula shook her head. "They're not quite that sophisticated. I'll hold our spot. Why don't you take Danny to see the kitties?"

Nellie looked at the corner doorway, marked "Kitten Room." "Okay," she agreed, swallowing her impatience. "C'mon, Dan my man."

Danny smiled wetly, arms extended. "Nuh, nuh, nuh!"

"You said 'Nellie,' didn't you? Did you hear him, Aunt Paula?"

"I think you're right," Paula agreed. "What a smart boy."

Nellie hugged his chunky warmth. The kid definitely had his moments.

She had to turn sideways to slip between the counter and stacked steel cat cages that had oozed out of the back rooms to crowd the lobby. "It's Raining Cats & Dogs—Please Spay & Neuter!" said a sign on the green-painted block wall.

The kitten room was quiet, most of the cats sleeping away the afternoon in their cages, piled three high on both sides. Danny reached for the gray-and-white kittens curled together in a purring clump in the nearest pen.

"Pretty kitties," Nellie agreed. Her eyes examined the room under the cold wash of fluorescent light.

So many cats—black, white, calico, gray—all sleeping on sheets of newspaper behind metal bars. Drains in the floor for hosing it all down.

"Mrr-ow."

Nellie walked back toward the door, following the voice. A huge gray tabby rubbed its head against the bars and purred.

"Mrr-ow," it said again, reaching a paw through an opening.

Ignoring the sign, "Keep Fingers Out of Cages," Nellie rubbed his head. "You're such a good kitty," Nellie told him. "Yes, you are. See the kitty, Danny."

She couldn't meet the cat's eyes. The information card on the door said he'd been surrendered because the owner "couldn't keep."

"Nellie!" Aunt Paula stuck her head around the corner.

"Coming."

Giving the cat a last ear scratch, Nellie returned to the lobby. She squeezed past a distressed woman with a cardboard box of puppies. "I don't know how you can call yourselves a humane society when you kill animals."

"We don't like it, either, but we have no choice, ma'am. There's just no more room here. If an animal's been here for sixty days, its time is up. Someone else walks in the door, every single day, with more animals for us. Where on earth can we put them?"

The woman shook her head. "I won't leave these innocent babies here—not to be killed." She made her way to the door with the big box. "They may just be animals, but they have some rights, too."

Nellie, handing Danny back to Aunt Paula, stared after the woman. The young, bearded man behind the counter smiled without humor. "It's a sad fact of life. It's not the animal's fault their owners aren't responsible and can't be bothered. But the animals die and the people walk away. What can I do for you ladies?"

Paula explained about Dooley. "We're looking for any information from when he came in."

The man was shaking his head even as she spoke. "I remember the dog. There was just nothing. I came in at 7:30 to feed, and he was tied to the doorknob."

"No notes?"

"Nope. And no collar, no license, no tags, no leash. Just a rope around his neck—and a flea collar."

Nellie pushed down discouragement. "Do you still have the rope or flea collar?"

The man shook his head again. He reached past Nellie to accept papers from an impatient woman behind them. "I'll be right with you, ma'am."

"It was just ordinary, light rope—like clothesline. And a typical flea collar. They went straight into the trash."

"Which day did he come in?"

"Monday. Definitely. I come in after the weekend and there he is. Jumped right up on me. Another time it was a box of kittens. People are always dumping on a Sunday night."

Nellie's eyes pleaded with him. "Anything else? How did he look?"

The man shrugged. "Healthy. Glad to see a friendly face. His nails were clipped and he was already neutered. Usually we have to do that here."

He seemed to reflect. "You know, people who neuter their dogs are usually responsible enough to make arrangements themselves if they can't keep the animal. They're not the type to drop thcm off."

Nellie tried to fit the image of a responsible dog owner with child abuse and abandonment. She couldn't make them fit together.

"No collar, though?"

Again, he shook his head. "Maybe he was a stray. He might have gotten lost and somebody else just found him and brought him here."

"Excuse me." The man reached past her to return the woman's papers. "You're going to need a check for the fee, plus spaying. See the list on the wall? Let me finish up here, then I'll be with you."

He turned back to Nellie. "Sorry. I need to check some people out here."

"That's okay. One last thing—have you noticed a teenage girl around here? About so tall, dark hair?" Nellie described the girl from the mall.

"Doesn't ring a bell with me. Sorry."

Nellie thanked him and had started toward the door when another thought stopped her. She turned and called back. "How old would you say the dog was? And how old do they have to be to be neutered?"

15

Discouragement and Hope

The bell on the door of the Perfect Pet grooming shop jingled as Nellie walked out. She shifted her library books to shove the Polaroid photo of Dooley into her purse.

"That's it," Peggy said. "That's the only grooming place in the phone book."

"She probably clipped Dooley's nails at home." Nellie fought discouragement. "The guy in there said lots of people do."

Monday 5:00 o'clock traffic—three pickups, a van, and two cars—rolled by on Market, Begg City's main street. That was pretty much the extent of rush hour. Waiting for the light to change, Nellie stared gloomily at a cut-out turkey in a Pilgrim hat on the dime store window. Why were those stupid birds always smiling?

"What now?" Peggy asked, stepping down when the little green walking man flashed on the sign.

"A bunch of things. First, we'll go meet Rick at Davey Dee's—see if we can get a lead on that girl. Then, I was thinking we should get something of Baby Jane's for Dooley to sniff, see if he recognizes the scent. After that—"

Peggy shook her head. "Mom's picking us up in—" She glanced at her wrist. "An hour and a half. If she hadn't been taking Grandpa to the mall for his new glasses, she'd have waited for us. The only reason we got to be out at all was to pick up this stuff from the library to do our papers. And we've got an algebra test the day after tomorrow."

"Don't remind me. I could study all night and still pull a D."

"That's because you tune out. You look at the stuff, but your brain leaves the building."

"I can't help it," Nellie told her. "It's self-defense. Anyway, we don't have to do all that other stuff tonight. I'm just saying as soon as we can."

The lower part of the coffee shop windows were steamed, but Nellie spotted Rick at a table toward the back. She pushed open the door to a breath of warm, french-fry-scented air.

In back there was a noisy family dining room. Crossing the even noisier front room where the teenagers always loafed, Nellie groaned and pointed. "Catch the curtains."

"Geese and windmills," Peggy said. "Love it."

In his never-ending attempt to create the perfect combination family restaurant and cool teen hangout, Davey took some decorating risks. The latest pairing of country curtains and Elvis Presley photos was as daring as it got.

"Hi." Nellie slid into a chair under a fading concert poster of Sam the Sham and his Pharaohs, who'd probably wowed them back in the '60's. She looked around. "Boy, there's no one at all here from Indian Camp School."

"Well, it's a week night. Nobody'd be over here unless they were at the library or something," Rick said. He pushed aside the honeycomb fold-out turkey to pass a basket of onion rings their way.

"What did you find out?" he asked.

"Zip. I guess now we'll have to start checking the vets for neutering records, but there's a lot more of them than grooming places."

"Seventeen," Peggy contributed, hooking four onion rings with her finger. "I checked the phone book. But a couple are all the way down by the state line."

Nellie sagged in her chair. She watched Peggy eat each ring in turn.

"It's a long shot anyway, Nell," Rick said. "First of all, you're only guessing that dog has anything to do with the baby. Second, he could've been neutered in another state for all you know."

"All we can do is try," she grumbled. "If you have a better idea, let me know."

Peggy waved at the waitress, pointing at Rick's glass. She held up two fingers. "Did you ask around here about the girl?"

"Yeah. I didn't get real far. That description pretty much fits a lot of kids."

"Who'd you ask? Just kids?"

He shook his head. "No. I talked to the waitress and Davey, too."

"So all we can do is sit around and drink Cokes night after night and hope she shows up?" Peggy asked.

"*I* can't sit here every night," Rick said. "And there's at least a couple other places where she could hang out. I asked."

The waitress brought their drinks. Nellie and Peggy counted out change and handed it to her.

As she walked away, Nellie stared after her. Rain streaked the light streaming from the pole outside the big windows.

"She might just go home after school, too," Peggy mused. "Or have band practice or a part-time job."

"I know." Nellie couldn't keep the frustration out of her voice. "And maybe she doesn't even go to school. Maybe she's a dropout. But all we can do is try." It seemed she kept saying that lately.

"Maybe we should split up," Rick said. "Each of us hang out somewhere different. If we all go trooping to the same place, it'll take forever."

"Not me," Peggy said. "I'm not walking into some place all by myself and sit around drinking sodas for an hour. That's no fun. Besides, people think you're a real loser—like you don't have any friends."

"We're not doing this for *fun*, Peggy." Nellie

couldn't blame her, though. Her own parents, she realized uneasily, would never let her troop all over town alone if they knew.

"I guess I could go alone and you girls go together," Rick said, grabbing his last onion ring before Peggy could snag it.

"Let's face it." Nellie looked at them. "I don't know about you, but my folks aren't going to let me go detecting every night, anyway."

"Well, that was kind of my point," Rick said. "If we only get to do this once or twice a week, it's stupid not to split up."

He was right. Nellie pushed aside that uncomfortable feeling and put on her pleading look, like Lady sitting by the grill at the church picnic. "Peggy?"

Peggy's cheeks got red—a sure sign of one of her stubborn attacks. She looked down at the basket and shook all the salt to one side. With a damp fingertip, she picked some up and put it in her mouth.

"Please, Peggy?"

"No. I won't do it." She picked up more salt.

Nellie pulled the basket away. "They use that stuff to melt ice on the roads. It'll kill you."

"Look," Rick said. "Why don't you think about it? Okay? You don't have to decide now."

Peggy didn't say a word. Her look, chin raised, said she'd already decided.

Nellie checked the wall clock. Since Mickey Mouse had died on him, Davey had replaced him with a rhinestone-studded cat with eyes and tail that went back and forth. "Hey, we've got an hour before Mrs. Penwick comes for us," she said. "Let's at least go see if we can get something of Baby Jane's for Dooley to sniff. She's only about two blocks back of here."

"May as well," Rick agreed, grabbing his jacket off the back of his chair.

"All right." Peggy's voice wasn't exactly enthusiastic, but she added, "I haven't seen the baby since that day at the church."

Nellie shivered as they stepped onto the wet sidewalk. Peggy put up her mini-umbrella, which was covered with purple, red, and yellow tulips.

Nellie huddled under it, rain coursing over her left shoulder. At least her head would be dry. Rick plodded beside them, his jacket hood turning dark under the streetlight as the rain hit it.

Begg City was bigger than Chestnut Grove, where they went to school. But it wasn't really a city.

Behind Davey Dee's parking lot, the houses started. Nobody said anything as they squished along. Nellie's socks were already damp.

They turned at the corner. Mrs. Carnahan's house was halfway down on the right.

Framed by the misty cone of light from the pole at the end of the block, a slight figure walked away from them. Head down, it paused at the corner.

The head lifted and looked to the right. "I think it's her!" Rick gasped.

16

A Chase

"Hey!" Rick yelled. "Wait up."

The girl turned at his voice, then ran.

"Wait!" Rick called. "We just need to talk."

She had a big head start on them. Nellie heard the wet slap of the girl's feet hitting the sidewalk ahead. She could really run.

Rick threw down his bookbag. Nellie jumped over the trailing strap and followed him.

His long legs and hours of basketball carried him faster than Nellie. Gradually he ran beyond her reach and started gaining on the fleeing girl.

"Please don't run!" he screamed, but the rain seemed to soak into the words, pulling them down. "We only want to talk."

She turned left at the next corner, heading uphill. Nellie, panting along a half-block behind Rick, could no longer see her.

Rick pivoted like he did on the basketball court, skidding on the rain-slicked pavement.

Then he too disappeared.

"Nellie!" The wail made her look back.

Peggy jogged halfheartedly, the way a cow does if it's forced. "Stop!"

Though Nellie scanned ahead to the now-empty corner where Rick and the girl had vanished, she slowed down. She couldn't catch up to them, anyway.

Peggy limped toward her. "I feel a blister."

"That's because your socks are wet," Nellie told her, swiping at her own soggy bangs.

Peggy stopped. She held her tulip umbrella like Mary Poppins, waiting to float skyward. All the gasping and puffing kind of spoiled the effect, though. So did the sodden tennis shoes.

She sniffled. "Did you get a look at her?"

Nellie shook her head. "Just a dark shape running away."

"Maybe it's not even her."

"She did run. There must be a reason."

Peggy dug a rumpled tissue from her pocket and blew her nose. "I'd run if a bunch of people started chasing me down a dark street."

Nellie squinted toward the corner where Rick and the girl had turned. "Let's at least walk up that way," she begged.

Peggy sighed. "All right."

Nellie sighed too. They might catch up to Rick at this rate, but only if he walked backward.

When they reached the streetlight, Nellie saw them. Rick was coming back down the hill, the girl beside him.

She looked scared to death, ready to run again if she got the chance. Nellie's heart began to pound.

They all stopped under the light. The girl was swallowed up in a big jacket, her dark hair pulled back. Her eyes were surprisingly light— blue or maybe gray. Despite the makeup, she looked chalk-white.

Was she fourteen? Fifteen? Was this what a child abuser looked like? To Nellie, this girl looked more like the victim.

"This is Jessica Landis," Rick said. "She has a problem."

Nellie shivered as cold air caught her damp pantlegs. "Problem" seemed a huge understatement for what this girl had.

"Did you leave that baby at the church nursery?" Nellie asked bluntly.

The girl—Jessica—drew a breath. "Look, please. You've got to understand."

Nellie noticed she didn't say, "What baby? What nursery?"

"Understand what?" Nellie exploded. "How you could dump an innocent baby on Peggy and me and take off for never-never land? How you could break her leg?"

Jessica was shaking her head. "No. No." She licked her lips, eyes darting toward Nellie's face but not quite meeting her glance. "Look, I'm late," Jessica said, hiking her backpack higher onto one shoulder. "So I've got to run, but that isn't my baby."

Rick put his hand on her arm. "Jessica." His voice was gentle. "You can't keep it a secret anymore. It's wrong."

Even the rain couldn't camouflage the girl's tears. Her shoulders shook.

Nellie stole a look at Peggy, standing stone-faced beneath the tulip umbrella. Then she looked at Rick, raising her brows in question.

He nodded slightly at Jessica, as if to say, "It's up to her."

The way she was crying, Nellie figured it might be awhile. "Should we head back toward Davey Dee's?" Nellie suggested, shivering as she wiped the film of fine droplets from her face.

"No point catching pneumonia," Rick agreed.

"I can't." Jessica's voice caught on a sob. "I have to go home."

"Jessica, please. You owe it to the baby," Rick said. "We don't want to get you into trouble, but everything's already a mess. If we found you, the police are going to find you."

The girl wiped a hand across her face. "You didn't find me," she argued. "You just happened to run into me and recognize me. Please," she begged. "I didn't do anything wrong."

"What *did* you do?" Nellie was surprised how hard her voice sounded.

"All right. You know so much—what's right, what's wrong. I'll tell you. You come down here, out of the rain."

17

Jessica's Story

A darkened house stood on the corner nearest Davey Dee's. It was a yellow Victorian with lacy white trim and a wraparound porch. One front pillar held a "For Sale" sign. The street light lit the closest end of the porch.

They all clumped up the steps after Jessica. Peggy shook out her umbrella and set it by the railing.

Following Jessica's lead, each slid down to sit on the floor, back against the wall. Tall holly bushes, still leafy, hid them from passing headlights.

Nellie was shaking now from cold, and her teeth were chattering. She drew her knees up and hugged them. Next to her, Peggy did the same.

"Okay," Jessica said. She was sitting on Nellie's other side, with Rick beside her. "You tell me what you'd do."

The girl looked straight ahead, eyes on the street lamp. The light shone on her face and glittered in the raindrops misting her clumped, wet bangs.

She blinked. "I babysit for people in the neighborhood. One of them was Mrs. Peterson. She's extremely young and divorced, and she's having a tough time.

"Mrs. Peterson has a daughter, five months old, named Lizbeth. Mrs. Peterson calls her 'the eye that never sleeps.' She's just awake all the time and restless."

Jessica rubbed her nose. "For a while, Mrs. Peterson called me like every week, but—uh—I think money was tight, because lately she was only calling every two or three weeks."

"And this Lizbeth was the baby at the church nursery?" Peggy interrupted before Nellie could jab her. "Mom gets mad when we're late," Peggy responded to Nellie's glare. "I'm just trying to cut through some of this."

Jessica ignored them. "Anyway, I knew something wasn't right because I found bruises on Lizbeth's arms and on her knee and ankle. And a few weeks ago, Mrs. Peterson didn't answer my knock, so I just went in. She was really shaking the baby."

Nellie shivered again.

"I stepped back into the hall and called her name again so she wouldn't know I saw her," Jessica said. "She was hugging Lizbeth when she came out, and her eyes were all red and puffy."

Fresh tears started rolling down Jessica's cheeks. "I didn't know what to do. She really loves Lizbeth. I know she does, but she just can't handle raising her alone.

"I was afraid to report her. I wouldn't want her to go to jail. I kept thinking, 'That could be me.' But what if something awful happened to Lizbeth?" Jessica darted a look at Nellie, then at Rick.

She turned back to Nellie and Peggy. "I was so afraid I'd open up the newspaper and see some horrible story and feel it was my fault for not doing something."

"Look," Nellie said. "When a little baby's in danger, I don't see any big issue about what to do. You report it."

Jessica leaned into Nellie's face. "Sure, that sounds so easy when you're not the one who has to pick up the phone and do it. But number one—Mrs. Peterson's life would've been ruined. And number two—how many news stories have you seen where they take someone's kid away for child abuse? Then they turn around and send the kid right back into all that."

She had a point. Nellie had seen those stories, too.

"So you kidnapped her?" Peggy frowned in the half-light.

"Don't say that!"

"Well, what would you call it?" Peggy asked. "Aren't you telling us you took the baby?"

"I did what I had to do. I typed a note from 'A

117

Concerned Neighbor' and said, 'I know you don't mean to hurt the baby, but you are. I'm taking her to a safe place. If you try to get her back, I'll have to tell on you.' I left it in the apartment when I took Lizbeth."

"How did you do all that without her catching you?" Rick asked.

Jessica slid farther down the wall. "Actually, it was easy. She left the baby alone pretty often. She wouldn't leave her real long, but like to run down to the store. She went to buy a paper just about everyday—to check the want-ads for jobs.

"I waited in the bushes at the side of the building till she left on Saturday, then zipped right in. The kitchen door up the back steps doesn't stay locked, and a lot of people know it."

"Did you plan all along to take her to the church?" Nellie asked.

Jessica dropped her eyes. "I didn't really know what I was going to do with her. I thought maybe—oh, I'd leave her on the steps at the police station. But it was too cold. And Lizbeth was crying and crying, even after I picked her up and cuddled her."

Nellie stared at the other girl, unable to imagine what it took to kidnap a baby. "Her leg was broken."

Jessica nodded. "Now I know. But there I was with this screaming baby, and I felt like I had to get rid of her before I got caught. And I remembered the sign in front of the church about the meeting and the free babysitting. I was in there once, and I knew that room was huge. I figured maybe I could slip her in the back without anyone noticing.

"I ran most of the way over. It was getting dark, and with me jogging up and down, Lizbeth finally dozed off. She woke up screaming as soon as I put her down, but by then I was out the door."

"Thanks." Peggy's voice oozed sarcasm. "Nellie and I were the 'free babysitting.' "

"I know. Rick told me, and I'm sorry I dumped on you. But I was desperate."

For a moment nobody spoke. A car swished by on the wet pavement, and a twig fell against the porch railing. Peggy sneezed.

"Has she been looking for the baby? Asked you if you know anything?" Nellie said.

Jessica shook her head. "Nobody's seen her that I know of, but she always did keep to herself. I think when she broke Lizbeth's leg, it scared her. She knew she couldn't keep her. It was too dangerous. And by evening the report was on the news. She had to know it was Lizbeth."

Rick ran a hand through his thick clump of dark hair. It was how he reacted to huge messes, which this certainly was.

"Have you told your parents?" he asked.

"My parents are idiots."

18

A Walk in the Dark

Nellie shifted on the hard porch floor, hugging her knees with both arms and looking at Jessica. The girl just stared at the light and wiped at her eyes.

Was she a hero? A criminal? A liar? And there was that same question—what should they do now?

"How close does Mrs. Peterson live?" Rick asked.

"Couple blocks. This isn't Los Angeles."

That explained the absence of palm trees, then—and why Nellie was freezing her nose off at the moment.

"Can you show us?" Nellie asked.

"Yeah, I guess." Gold hoop earrings swung forward as Jessica climbed to her feet. "Gotta make it quick, though."

They trooped down the steps into the lamplight. The rain had stopped, but the air still felt like wet socks.

Jessica caught Nellie's arm. "No police, okay?"

Nellie looked down. How could she answer a question like that?

"I didn't do anything wrong," the girl insisted, this time to Rick. Then why did it feel wrong? Nellie wondered. Why did they have to slink around in the dark?

Jessica kept walking, anyway. Peggy, Mary Poppins umbrella refolded, did too, but she didn't look particularly happy about it.

The apartment house on South Woods Street was a three-story Victorian-looking brick, with an entryway in front and bow windows up both sides. The second-floor window Jessica pointed to was dark.

Two big hemlock trees dripped on either side of the front walk. They hung all the way to the ground.

"A little on the creepy side, isn't it?" Rick asked.

Jessica shrugged. "It's better in the daytime."

Nellie walked to the door. Seven little tin mailboxes lined the left side. The light bulb above them was burned out.

The light on the right still worked. Beneath it were buzzers. There were no names on the yellowed cards beside each one, just apartment numbers. Even they were hard to read. The light bulb couldn't have been more than forty watts.

"Cheap landlord, huh?" Nellie asked.

"Definitely," Jessica said. "He lives in Pittsburgh and just collects the rent by mail. But the rent's pretty cheap, too, Mrs. P. always says."

"Which is her apartment?" Nellie asked.

"Number 2-A—Hey! Don't push that!"

Nellie had already pressed the buzzer. Jessica shoved at her. "What did you do that for?" she demanded.

"I—I guess I wanted to see if anyone was home. I wanted to see her."

Nellie had to admit she had nothing to say if Mrs. Peterson answered the buzzer. She only half-heard Jessica's angry muttering as the girl slipped into the shadow of the hemlock.

Nellie's stomach rocked like a canoe getting passed by a motorboat. But the outside buzzer was silent, and nobody came to the door.

"Hey, Nellie, Rick. Look here." Peggy, who'd hung back, pointed at a small wooden sign on the patch of frostbitten lawn near the sidewalk.

Nellie followed Rick. The sign said, "Apartment for Rent—No Children. No Pets."

"Ha!" Rick said. "I guess when you live in the city, you can make whatever rules you want, but people are pretty much going to ignore you."

"I wonder if it's Mrs. Peterson's apartment. Maybe she took off," Nellie said. She chewed at her lip.

"When's the last time you talked to her?" she called to Jessica.

Her only answer was the spattering of rain from the trees as the wind shifted. "Hey!" Nellie yelled, walking toward the shadows where Jessica had been hiding.

Rick and Peggy followed, fanning across the wet grass and softly calling the girl's name. Peggy blew her nose on a raggedy tissue. "She's gone."

"She must've run off as soon as you rang that bell," Rick said.

Nellie felt sick. "We had her. I'm so stupid. I could kick myself. The whole Mrs. Peterson thing could be a fairy tale, for all we know. And I let her get away."

Rick ran a hand through his hair. "Well, at least we've got her name and phone number for the police."

"I think she was telling the truth," Peggy said. "The way she was crying and her voice kind of shook."

Nellie kicked furiously at a pebble. "If you're fifteen and you've abandoned your baby—your abused baby—and somebody catches you, that's enough reason to cry and shake."

"Look," Rick said cheerfully. "We've got a lot on her now. And she's right. It isn't LA. She ought to be easy enough for the cops to track down."

Nellie gnawed some more at her bottom lip. "If she *was* telling the truth, she might be right. Maybe the police are a mistake."

"Come on, Nellie. Don't be silly. Once you start keeping secrets from the police, you're heading for big trouble."

"At least let's think about it." She couldn't stand on a strange lawn and argue with Rick all night. "Till we get home."

Nellie was standing at the far side of the hemlock, looking up the hill. "I'll bet she went up the street."

There was a stone retaining wall along the edge of the lawn. The next yard sloped upward behind a tangle of bushes. Nellie ran a hand over the damp, mossy surface of the wall. She looked back along the side of the house.

A wooden stairway, with garbage cans beneath it, climbed to the second and third floors. Her heart began racing, like a motorcycle waiting at a stop light.

"Rick, Peggy!" Her voice sounded breathless, and she gulped.

"Aw, Nellie." Peggy seemed to know right away when Nellie had plans she wouldn't like. Or maybe she figured it was best to object automatically when Nellie used that tone of voice.

Nellie had also figured out that it was best to keep going when Peggy started planting her feet. It was probably a lot like owning a mule.

Nellie rubbed the spot where her heart was banging against her throat. "Remember she said the kitchen door wouldn't stay locked?"

19

Up the Darkened Steps

The stairway was unlit. Shadows fell on shadows.

"No breaking and entering." Rick's voice was sharp.

"No breaking," Nellie agreed. "Unlocked door —remember? And not really entering, either. Just peeking."

"Why?"

"Just to see if the apartment's empty. To see if that's the one for rent."

"We may not have to open the door for that," Rick said. "Most kitchen doors have windows."

"There you go," Nellie cheerfully agreed. "Just depends on how dark it is up there."

"Nellie!" Peggy grabbed her arm. "The police can check all that."

"Maybe." Nellie was still thinking about the police. "But they wouldn't tell us anything."

"How about we go up and knock?" Rick suggested. "No answer at the buzzer, so there's no harm trying at the back door. If the apartment runs all the way to the back of the building, maybe she's back there and just didn't hear us."

"Just knock." Peggy wanted the agenda clear. "Knock and peek."

"Right," Nellie agreed. "Knock and peek."

Nellie had to hustle as they started toward the back. Rick was in the lead—typical guy thing. But as they approached the intense dark beneath the stairs, it seemed like she had to breathe around her heart. Her palms were sweating despite the cold wind.

Whose apartment was it? Really?

The girl who called herself Jessica could have led them anywhere. They didn't know her, didn't know what was waiting at the landing above their heads. If someone could hurt her own baby, what might she do to them?

Hard curls of peeling paint scraped at Nellie's hand as she touched the railing. Low maintenance back here, too. A faint scent of garbage— stale and slightly orangey—floated over the wet smells of the yard.

Scrape, thump. Their feet sounded loud, but there was a TV chattering somewhere in the first floor apartment. Nellie tried to tiptoe.

She felt like she was dragging the mother of all laundry bags as she climbed the steps. Peggy clung to her back the whole way, occasionally gasping and giving a little tug. She was Nellie's own personal human airbrake.

The steps creaked underfoot. There was the landing, big enough for one person to stand.

All three crowded onto it. Nellie stepped onto the lower rung of the railing and hung on so she could breathe.

The landing was bare, except for a dead geranium that must have been forgotten at first frost.

Looking over Rick and Peggy's heads, Nellie could see the tiny window in the kitchen door. It was only a patch of black.

There was another pane of glass just past the landing—small and opaque-looking. Probably a bathroom. All the way back, another dark window stared out into the night.

Rick knocked, a sharp sound that made Nellie jump. They waited, but no one answered.

The wind shifted, rustling the dry bushes along the edge of the yard. Nellie shivered.

"Try once more," she told Rick, clinging to the railing with one hand and wrapping the other arm around herself for warmth.

He rapped a bit harder. Somewhere in the building a dog roused with a flurry of high-pitched yips.

Peggy pulled at Rick's sleeve. "Come on, we've got to go."

The dog kept yipping. "Come *on*," Peggy said, starting down the steps.

"She's right, Nell. Nobody's home and you can't see in. We don't want someone coming to find out why the dog's barking."

Rick followed Peggy onto the stairs. Nellie stepped back onto the landing.

The others were already halfway down, but she hesitated, reluctant to leave, not knowing. Cupping her hands around her eyes, Nellie peered through the glass.

It was like looking into someone's ear—nothing but darkness. Frustrated, Nellie grasped the doorknob. She looked down at her friends nearing the bottom of the stairs. Feeling sneaky, she gently turned the knob. The door swung open.

The apartment felt cold. The small sounds Nellie made—the rustle of her jacket, even her breathing—bounced off bare floors and walls.

It had a stale smell. Dead air.

"*Nellie!*" Peggy's voice shrilled from the yard. "What are you *doing?*"

The yipping became more frenzied. Now there was a new sound—like someone pelting a wall with beanbags. Nellie realized the dog was jumping at the door of one of the apartments.

"Nellie, get down here this instant!"

She pulled the door closed with another squawk and a click. Beneath her, Peggy hissed, "The dog's going to get you!"

Nellie came down, the yipping beanbag action ringing in her ears. *Oh, yeah, run for your life. Crazed killer Chihuahua on the loose.*

One thing now she knew. Mrs. Peterson—if she ever existed—sure didn't live here anymore.

20

A Plan of Attack

Nellie rolled onto her side to drop tissue into the wastebasket. The couch creaked.

She'd escaped the fearsome, crazed Chihuahua. But running around Begg City in a cold rain, with Peggy spewing cold germs, had brought Nellie down. She rubbed her head. It felt like an overheated watermelon getting ready to explode.

From the kitchen came the unending jingle of Danny's Happy Apple toy. Once she'd thought the sound was cheerful. But after a whole morning of it, she had started wondering how to turn the toy into Happy Applesauce.

Despite her hot head, Nellie shivered. She pulled the old, rainbow-striped afghan tighter. Even a day off from school wasn't worth this.

Mom was at the door. "Chamomile tea?"

"No thanks. Maybe some o.j. in a little bit. I'll come get it when I'm ready."

Nellie shut her eyes. The worst part of being sick was how muzzy-headed she was. Here she had a whole day to think through everything that had happened, but her brain kept fading.

Rick had called the police about Jessica—or at least he'd said he was going to. But she wondered if it would do them a lot of good.

As soon as Nellie'd gotten home, she'd tried the phone number Jessica had given them. It was answered by a service station.

A fake number. Nellie figured the name was probably a phony, too.

How much more had been a lie? Nellie agreed with Peggy. The story sounded like it might be true, or at least part of it. But what part?

She blew her nose again. Well, thanks to her lying, Jessica or whoever she was couldn't be warned about the police. So she was on her own.

And Nellie couldn't ask her whether "Mrs. Peterson" had a big, scruffy dog. She should have asked while they had her last night; now she couldn't.

The girl would probably have lied, anyway. So Nellie would just have to plod along from vet to vet, to all seventeen if necessary, hoping one of them recognized Dooley's mug shot. *If*, she reminded herself, *I can figure out a way Mom and Dad will let me go.*

Nellie sneezed and reached for the tissue box. She pulled out the last one and threw the box in the trash. She'd have to make her tissues-and-o.j. run before the next sneeze.

She swung her legs over the side and stood, bracing herself in case the floor pitched. She put out a hand to steady herself against the door frame and headed for the kitchen.

"How's the patient?" Mom beamed tearily over the onions she was chopping and throwing in a steaming pot.

"I can't smell the onions."

"Count your blessings. Want that juice now?"

"I'll get it." Nellie padded toward the fridge.

"Still disappointed in Dooley?"

Nellie set the juice on the table and went for a glass. The Happy Apple tinkled merrily from the playpen. She rubbed her aching head.

"Oh, Mom. I don't know whether he does or doesn't know the baby. He sniffed that T-shirt like he was interested, but then he acted pretty much the same with Danny's."

"Well, he does know Danny, too."

"Yeah, but the only thing he really went crazy for was the granola bar wrapper in my pocket."

"Can you blame him?" Mom grinned. "I'd rather smell a granola bar than a used T-shirt, myself, and I don't have his keen sense of smell."

Nellie flopped into a chair and sipped the sweet, flavorless juice. *Lassie would have done better*, she thought.

"This whole thing's driving me crazy."

"Honey, it's not your problem anymore." Mom stepped over the chew toys Danny had flung onto the floor. Nellie had once hoped the house would get tidier with Mom home all the time, but actually it was worse.

"I know that," Nellie said. "But it's so embarrassing. Everyday somebody at school mentions it. A couple kids are mean about it, but mostly they're kidding."

"Ignore the mean ones, Nellie. I don't have to tell you that. And when people kid you, just laugh. They don't mean to hurt you."

"It doesn't help that they're kidding," Nellie muttered. "I don't want to talk about it."

"But you yourself won't let it go."

Nellie rested her head on her hand. "I can't."

Danny threw his Happy Apple. It hit the floor with a thunk.

"Guess it's naptime," Mom said. She picked him up, a drool streamer trailing behind.

He grinned and waved his arms at Nellie as they went past. Nellie had to smile back.

A typical baby. A typical day with a typical baby. Had Nellie worn her folks out like this? She guessed she had. But then, they'd probably done the same to their parents.

And the smiles were part of it, too. Nellie was noticing that most things in life seemed to work that way. You didn't get to go down the cafeteria line and just pick the parts you liked.

Lady stuck a wet nose into Nellie's hand. Nellie looked into the dog's brown eyes.

"Can somebody be good to their dog and hurt their own baby?"

Lady put up a paw and Nellie rubbed behind the dog's ears.

The phone rang. "Nellie?" Rick's voice sounded stuffy, too. "How're you feeling?"

"Okay for something that should've died yesterday."

"You think you'll feel all right to go check some vets tomorrow after school?"

"Sure. I can handle it." Nellie steadied herself against the ledge and blew her nose.

"Either tomorrow or the day after," Rick said. "My cousin Jay said he'd take us."

Nellie frowned. "The guy with the hair?"

Rick laughed. "He's okay. I help him work on his car sometimes, and he owes me."

"All right. If Mom lets me. Did you talk to the police about Jessica the escape artist?"

"They're looking for her. If she lives in that neighborhood, they'll find her."

"Which she must," Nellie said. "Or she wouldn't have been walking around there."

"They'll check on the apartment, too. Whether she was telling the truth or not, it was a great break, running into her."

"I guess." Nellie tried to feel that way too, but doubt clung to her.

"And we know Dooley had to have been neutered in about the past six months, so if you're right about him, that's a good clue, too."

"I'm right." Deep inside, Nellie was sure. But could she feel triumph when she solved the mystery and brought them all back together again? If Jessica was right, Nellie might have to live with the regret for the rest of her life.

21

On the Trail of a Dog

Although Nellie's cold kept her home another day, she began to feel pretty good by evening. Somehow she and Rick had forgotten that evening was youth group.

As disappointed as she was not to be able to talk to the vets on their list, Nellie nevertheless felt a twinge of relief. "I'm still tired," she admitted to Peggy as they helped set up folding chairs.

"Not to mention," Peggy muttered, looking to make sure Rick wasn't within earshot, "I wouldn't be in any hurry to cruise around with that bizarro."

"Jay's okay," Nellie insisted. "He's Rick's cousin. He just wears his hair a little different."

"A little. He looks like he's leading a war party. How many people do you know with their heads shaved except for a little ponytail sticking up on top?"

"You can't judge by people's looks," Nellie

said. All the same, she had to admit riding around with Jay tomorrow night wasn't exactly at the top of her wish list. And she still hadn't brought herself to ask Mom.

Once Mom had had Jay in her Sunday school class. She always said he was a "dear boy." Somehow, though, Nellie suspected Mom wouldn't be delighted to send her on the road with him. Especially in that car of his—a decrepit purple Volkswagen Beetle.

The meeting, Nellie soon decided, wasn't much improvement over cruising the county with Jay. First they got into a big discussion over how people hadn't shown up to help at the Begg City Church.

After that, everybody just seemed to start talking about Baby Jane, the police investigation, and child abuse generally. "I think if they ever find that mother, they should throw away the key," Kathy Bauer pronounced.

"We don't know the whole story," Nellie insisted uncomfortably. "We're not the judge."

Kathy snorted. "What's to judge? Somebody abuses a baby, then abandons it. Case closed."

"Do you know something we don't, Nellie?" Heather asked, curiosity in her gray eyes.

Nellie shook her head. She couldn't explain about Jessica and Mrs. Peterson and Dooley—about all the things she'd been thinking.

"It makes you wonder," Ron said. He was a nice guy, quiet and good in school. "Sometimes I think it might be better if people like that never had babies. I know abortion's wrong, but—"

"I know," Heather agreed. "Wouldn't it be better for the baby to go straight to Jesus than suffer the way they do when their parents don't want them?"

Nellie shifted on the hard metal chair, looking at Rick, who wouldn't be sitting there if his mother had felt that way. He raked a hand back through his dark forelock and leaned forward, eyes glittering.

"Since when do we get to decide which wrong thing's better? And anyway, just how do you figure a baby doesn't suffer in an abortion?"

Nellie never liked to say much in a group. Her heart started pounding in her throat, knowing she had to speak up.

Peggy's voice surprised her. "Rick's right. That choice is for God, not us."

"What's easier isn't the point," Nellie agreed. "Killing's killing. I don't notice anybody saying it's okay to give poison gas to a sleeping baby, just because it's easier on the baby than abuse."

The discussion troubled Nellie. In her mind, it all seemed tangled with the right and wrong of finding Baby Jane's mother.

That night she curled into a ball under the quilts and prayed about it. "Father, it all seems clear to other people, but I need your help here. They say it's wrong to put puppies to sleep, but okay to kill human babies that haven't been born yet if you don't want them.

"Then they say a mother who hurts her baby

once it's born should be locked up. They don't even ask why she did it, or think she may not have meant to do it, or maybe she needs help.

"Father, Janie's *here*. But she's hurt, and her mom probably did it. Is it a mistake to look for her mom? Will they lock her up? Or will they give Janie back and let her be hurt again?"

When Nellie finally slept, anxious dreams churned through her mind. But she woke feeling clearer.

"Two wrongs still don't make a right," she told Lady. "Janie—or Lizbeth—has a right to know her parents, and they have a responsibility to her."

But Nellie knew that whoever had hurt Janie was hurting too. Just finding the baby's mother wasn't enough. Nellie had to be sure whoever it was would get help so she could do the right thing. Mrs. Carnahan would probably know about that—if it wasn't already too late.

"Our records aren't kept that way," the veterinary receptionist told them, pushing Dooley's mug shot back across the counter. "If you had an owner's name and address, we could check the files."

Nellie's heart skidded. "But that's the problem," she repeated. "We're trying to find that out. Can we explain?"

The brisk-looking woman was already turning to settle a young man's bill for his cat. "It's important," Nellie pleaded.

The receptionist's sigh carried clearly. "Honey, this is our busiest time of day. Everybody comes in after work and school."

"That's all right," Rick told her. "We'll come back another time."

"We've neutered hundreds of animals in the last six months," the woman told him, not even looking up. "This is a big practice."

"Thank you. We'll come back," Rick repeated.

The door jingled as Peggy pulled it shut behind them. Nellie stamped down the steps in frustration. This had been their first try. "If all seventeen vets are like this, we may as well forget it!"

"They won't be," Rick assured her. "Besides, there are only five vets actually close to Begg City. I don't really think we'll have to check the ones that are way out."

"Speaking of 'way out,' " Peggy muttered near Nellie's ear. "I'm glad your folks said 'no' about going with Jay."

"They didn't really say 'no.' It's just that Dad said he'd take us."

Dad was waiting in their ancient station wagon, reading the newspaper by the light from the pole lamp. "No luck," Nellie told him, sliding into the backseat. "We have to try someplace else."

"One more," Dad said. "It's kind of intriguing, thinking maybe we'll find out where Dooley came from. But when you come down to it, it's a long shot—and it's getting close to suppertime."

He turned the ignition key, and the old car

coughed and gasped to life. "What if that's the place that operated on him?" Peggy asked, looking back as they drove across the lot.

"Well, we'll just have to try them again when they're not so busy," Nellie said. But with school everyday, when would that be?

"Where to?" Dad asked.

Rick gave him the address and they talked about how to get there. It was out on the main route near the shopping mall.

"This will have to be the last one for tonight," Rick agreed with Dad. "It's already getting dark."

"If we could just do one more, we'd only have two of the nearby ones for next time," Nellie pleaded. She put one hand on his shoulder and one on Dad's. "Don't forget we're going to have to go back to The Dog and Cat Clinic. The more we can squeeze in now, the better."

Dad squinted at his watch, then met her eyes in the rearview mirror. "Let's just see how this one goes, okay?"

Dr. Mandelbaum's Pet Hospital, a low white building with slate blue shutters, crouched between a row of houses and the Sears Automotive Center. There were rust-colored bushes by the front steps. Apparently they'd been "watered" once too often by the patients.

Dad parked between the only two cars in the lot and opened his paper. As they stepped out, Nellie filled her lungs with cold air. Even laced with exhaust from the automotive center, it smelled better than their mildewed upholstery.

"At least this place isn't so crowded," Peggy commented.

"But then, they probably don't neuter as many dogs," Nellie said, fighting rising discouragement.

Dr. Mandelbaum's door didn't jingle. When Rick opened it, he had to shove it past a sticking spot in the swollen frame.

The empty waiting room featured a sofa and two chairs covered in bright orange vinyl. Tan stuffing oozed from a triangular rip in the couch back.

There was no receptionist here. Yipping poured steadily from behind a claw-marked door at the rear.

"I guess we just sit down and wait," Rick finally said, sinking onto the edge of a chair.

Peggy sat, too, but Nellie walked around. She studied cat and dog photos and a color poster of the life-cycle of the flea. After awhile she sat too.

Peggy had the only magazine, a ragged and coverless copy of *Cat Fancy*. Nellie looked at Rick, then at the carpet. It was the color of a boxer that needed a bath. Several stains spread like continents at her feet.

Maybe it wasn't even worth waiting here. Nellie had just looked up to ask what Rick thought when the inner door opened.

A bearded man came out. Next to him plodded a silver-muzzled cocker spaniel. "Give those to Missy until they're gone," said the stocky, gray-haired woman in the turquoise lab coat.

Her eyes widened as she looked around at Nellie and the others. "You have a pet, yes?"

"No—I mean, yes," Nellie said. "I mean, that's not why we're here."

The woman gestured to the back room. "Well, why don't you come in and we'll talk, yes? I'm Dr. Mandelbaum and you are—?"

Rick introduced them.

"Through here," the vet said, leading them past a cramped examination room and into a more cramped office.

"Just move those magazines off the chairs, darlings."

Nellie picked up a stack of advertising, veterinary journals, and boxes of samples to set it on the floor. As she did, a yelp and a hiss from beneath her chair made her jump.

"Oh, that's Marco!" the vet said. "He was nearly killed by a garbage truck, but the driver—such a nice man—brought him here. Marco's tail is dead now, but otherwise he's fine. He lives here and is in charge of everything."

Marco, a meaty, orange tabby, leapt from floor to table to the top of the file cabinet. He sat scowling, his tail dangling straight down.

"Just put that clutter anywhere, darlings." Dr. Mandelbaum sank into the saggy desk chair, took a sip of coffee from a mug that said, "The More I See of Some People, the More I Like My Dog."

"Pah! Cold." She made a face. "I'm semi-retired now. Don't have anybody to file this stuff—" she gestured "—or heat my coffee. I'd close the place up, but the old ones would miss me."

"So you mostly just treat your old patients?" Peggy's voice echoed Nellie's discouragement.

"Yes, that's the way it goes. People don't want a vet that's only got office hours once a week." Dr. Mandelbaum chuckled. "But I'm here everyday, anyway. Always there's an emergency."

"I guess you remember all your patients then," Nellie said, thinking at least they could eliminate this place pretty quickly.

"Oh, my goodness, yes. I've known most of them since they were kitties and puppies. But now, what can I do for you, my darlings?"

Nellie pulled Dooley's picture from her purse. "Do you know this dog?"

Dr. Mandelbaum adjusted smudged eyeglasses and took the photo. Nellie laced her fingers together, trying not to hope the vet would say, "Oh, that dog belongs to a girl called Jessica Landis," or "That's Mrs. Peterson's dog."

Happy recognition flooded the woman's face. "It's Barney!"

Rick, Peggy, and Nellie exchanged an excited look. "Are you sure?" Rick asked.

"Sure? Look at that precious face. Who could forget it? Even though," she admitted, "I haven't seen him for awhile."

Nellie's heart was thumping. "He was picked up as a stray, and we've been looking for the owner."

142

Dr. Mandelbaum chuckled. "People's names I'm not so hot with. Let me check his file."

The vet pushed herself out of the chair with some effort and turned to the battered, gray metal file cabinet in the corner. Marco looked down, studying her head with interest.

Flipping through folders, she muttered, "Dogs, dogs. Baby, Banner, Barkley, Barney. Here we go."

She pulled the thin manila folder and brought it back to the desk. "Shots and neutering; that's all I did. Oh, yes. How could I forget Ms. Salera?"

Nellie's stomach did a nosedive. She'd been so sure Dooley had lived with Janie, so sure his picture would lead them to her mother. Had Jessica lied about her name, too? Or did Dooley belong to someone altogether different—someone who might want to take him back from Aunt Paula?

22

Dooley Takes Action

"Miss Salera?" Nellie asked.

Dr. Mandelbaum nodded and closed the folder. She smiled once more at Dooley's picture, then pushed it back at Nellie.

"Yes. She was very big, you know?" The vet held out arms to indicate a round tummy. "We joked about whether I could deliver babies as well as puppies."

Nellie's heart jerked upward again. "Did you ever see her after the baby was born?"

Dr. Mandelbaum shook her head. "I wondered why—if something happened to Barney, or they'd moved, or found another vet. I so hoped everything was all right. Sometimes when there's a baby, a clumsy big dog is not so welcome anymore."

"Doctor, do you have an address?" Rick asked.

The vet pushed her glasses lower on her nose. "Let's see. That would be 215 South Woods

Street, Apartment 2-A. Ms. Sara Salera. Does that help?"

"It's a start," Nellie told her. "Thanks so much." She scrambled to her feet.

Dr. Mandelbaum touched Nellie's arm. "Barney—how is he?"

"He's fine, doctor." Nellie pulled Peggy toward the door. "Thanks again. You've been a big help."

Nellie was shivering by the time they stepped back out into the splash of light from the automotive center. The sky had already gone dull gray, and Dad had put down his paper and was drumming his fingers on the steering wheel.

"Jessica was telling the truth," Peggy said. "That was the apartment we went to. I guess Sara Salera is really Mrs. Peterson."

"Or the other way around," Nellie said. "If she was single, she could've given herself that married name to rent the apartment. Peterson sounds like the kind of nice, ordinary, respectable name you might pick if you wanted to assume that sort of identity."

Rick opened the door and they crawled in.

"Can we go to Aunt Paula's?"

Dad shook his head. "It's late."

"Yeah, I have to get home too, Nellie," Rick said. "We can call the police and give them this name. Let them take it from here."

"What did you find out?" Dad asked.

They all explained at once, with Dad shaking his head in disbelief. "Who'd have ever thought you'd really track him down?"

"Do you think they'll find Janie's mom now with that name?" Peggy asked.

"I don't know," Dad admitted. "But if it's her real name—or she's used it other places—it ought to help."

To Nellie, it seemed like too many "ifs."

The next day was Friday. With no more clues left to follow up, Nellie felt restless, her mind churning like a pump in a dry well. At lunch Rick vetoed her idea of calling to see if she could find a driver's license record for Sara Salera.

"The police do that stuff, Nell," he told her, forking a wad of mushy cafeteria spaghetti. "If they hear a kid on the phone, what do you think they're going to tell you?"

Nellie slumped in her seat, thinking how unfair everything was. If you were under eighteen, you were pretty much ignored or laughed at by anyone in authority—despite the fact that she and Peggy and Rick had turned up most of the good clues in this investigation so far.

"You're sleeping over at my place," Peggy reminded. "We can rent movies. We don't need to investigate anymore."

"*Plan 9 from Outer Space*?" Nellie asked sourly. Peggy loved to rent the worst of the low-budget movies and point out all the hokey details.

"It's a classic," Peggy insisted. "The set and the costumes are like right out of your basement."

"Why would I spend money to watch some-thing I could have produced in my cellar?"

"It's so bad it's good. Well, not good, really. But it's so bad it's funny."

Nellie only half-heard her. She was thinking about Sara Salera, who loved her dog and—according to Jessica—loved her baby, too.

Nellie remembered that she'd been planning to talk to Mrs. Carnahan about what would hap-pen to Janie—Lizbeth—if her mother was found. And what would happen to the mother.

On the bus ride home with Peggy, Nellie ex-plained. "I just need to talk to her, plus see the baby, of course."

"That's all?" Peggy's voice was wary.

"Well. . . ." Nellie looked out the window at the neat brick houses near Peggy's. The frost-faded lawns were trim, and most doors wore harvest wreaths.

"Nellie?" Peggy prodded.

Nellie turned back to her friend. "I know it sounds silly, but I'd really like to take Dooley. I want to see him with Janie—I mean Lizbeth. See if he reacts."

Peggy sighed. "Jessica said the baby came from that apartment. Dr. Mandelbaum said Dooley did, too. That's good enough for me."

"I know," Nellie said. "But that's—" She waved her hands, searching for the right word. "That's circumstantial evidence. Dooley's an eyewit-ness."

"Dooley's a dog," Peggy said, unimpressed.

"Besides, you saw him with that T-shirt. 'Eye-witless' is more like it."

"Look," Nellie said. "Lizbeth's mother ran away, and who knows where she went. If Dooley can recognize the baby, maybe he can help the police track Sara Salera, too."

At Peggy's snort of laughter, Nellie shook her head. Some people were never cut out to be detectives.

Dooley surged forward, jerking the leash in Nellie's hand. He inspected the curb with his nose, tail waving in excitement.

Light rain washed the streets of Begg City. As it penetrated Dooley's fur, it sent up a doggie aroma to clash with the rich scent of dying foliage.

A cold-edged gust caught at a big oak, loosening a few of the last limp, cinnamon-colored leaves. They swirled tiredly as they fell and stuck where they landed.

Nellie tugged at the leash. Unreasonably, she felt keyed-up, like she just couldn't wait for Dooley's nasal inspection of the sidewalk.

Beside her, Peggy patiently waited, protected by her rain shoes and tulip umbrella. As Dooley came up for air, he shook himself, sending dog-scented droplets over her arm and side.

Peggy jumped. "Oh, yuck!" Dooley grinned and trotted forward, pulling like Buck in *Call of the Wild*.

"You know, Mrs. Carnahan isn't going to want

that big, wet, smelly thing in her house."

"She likes dogs," Nellie assured her. "It's not like I didn't call and check first."

They turned the corner onto Mrs. Carnahan's street, Dooley still tugging and sniffing. This was the street where they'd met Jessica, only a block and a half from Davey Dee's—two blocks from the apartment building.

Dooley's ears pricked up. He must have walked here a hundred times, Nellie realized. This was where it all started, and where it all came back.

"Oh, rats!" Nellie recognized the bulky figure in chili-pepper-red high heels who was climbing Mrs. Carnahan's porch steps.

"What?"

"That's not exactly Avon calling," Nellie told Peggy. "That makeup lady in the beehive hair doesn't know when to give up. Mrs. Carnahan told me she's getting to be a nuisance."

Nellie hung back. She just didn't think she could handle a demonstration of "Cornbread Talcum Powder from our Village Bakeshop Collection."

"Maybe Mrs. Carnahan will send her away." Peggy wiped at her nose.

"She's too nice," Nellie said. "Beehive told her she's a widow, and she needs to sell that stuff to make a living."

"Let's wait over here, out of the rain," Peggy suggested, turning back to the porch where they'd sat with Jessica.

"Okay." Nellie pulled at the wet leash. "Come *on*, Dooley."

The dog's lunge caught her off-balance as she turned toward the porch. The leash slipped roughly through her fingers, and Dooley took off up the street.

"*Dooley!*"

Peggy screamed. "He's going to attack the makeup lady!"

"No!" Nellie said, though her voice wavered. He'd nipped at Aunt Paula, but surely he wouldn't go after a stranger.

Weak-kneed, Nellie ran after him. "Dooley, stop! *Dooley!*"

23

Dog Attack!

Beehive turned. Her eyes widened in horror.

"Dooley!" Nellie's shout came out in a sob.

The big dog charged, his paws slapping at the wet sidewalk and sending up spurts of water. The trailing leash bobbed against the pavement.

Dooley couldn't be doing this, but he was—and Nellie knew she'd never reach Mrs. Carnahan's porch in time to stop him.

Beehive had dropped her makeup case. She stood frozen at the door, panic on her face.

If only Mrs. Carnahan would come and let her in! But it was too late—Dooley cleared the steps in two great leaps.

Nellie stumbled, hurting her ankle. But she ran on. She had to do something. How do you stop a dog attack? Throw water?

When she reached the foot of the steps, Dooley was stretched up against the makeup lady. Wiggling all over, paws on her stomach, the dog was washing her face with his tongue.

A slurp attack! Relief came over Nellie in waves, leaving her shaking.

Nellie grabbed the leash in one hand and his collar with the other. "Dooley, get down."

She pulled Dooley off the woman briefly before he jumped up again. "I'm sorry," Nellie mumbled. "I don't know what got into him."

She pulled him down again. Dooley grinned and wagged and wiggled all over, droplets of slobber hitting the porch like big raindrops.

Beehive was shaking too. Her beehive—a wig—had been knocked sideways, revealing a knot of dark hair. Dooley's face wash had left one cheek scoured of makeup, and it looked pale next to the Sonora Sunset blazing on the other side.

"N-nice dog," Beehive said, nervously patting the air above his head. "Good b-baby." She shoved her helmet of pumpkin-colored hair back into place.

Peggy crept hesitantly up the steps, just as Mrs. Carnahan came to the door. "What on earth?"

"I'm so sorry," Nellie repeated. "Dooley just took off. He was drowning her in drool." She pulled a crumpled tissue from her pocket and began scrubbing at the paw marks on Beehive's lime-green coat.

The woman waved her away with hands that trembled. She laughed. "It's all right. Dogs always go for me."

She reached for her makeup case and Dooley licked her hand. He gave a short bark, his tail whipping the air in a frenzy of joy.

"Good boy," Beehive said, giving him a quivering smile as she released her case for a moment and patted his head. He grinned back at her, an all-wet grin with red tongue and sharp white teeth.

"I guess it's that blasted Bakeshop Collection," Beehive said. "What can you expect when you go around smelling like food?"

"Come in, everyone," Mrs. Carnahan said. "You'll want to freshen up and rest a minute."

Beehive scooped up her makeup case. "Oh no, thank you. I'll just be going now. I'll get myself home and change out of this coat. It's all right," she repeated, patting the general direction of Dooley's head again.

She smiled weakly at Nellie, darting her a quick glance that only reached neck-level. *Poor woman*, Nellie thought, glimpsing the sparkle of tears in her eyes.

"Are you sure?" Mrs. Carnahan said. "You've had a terrible fright."

Nellie wasn't sure how much Mrs. Carnahan had seen, but she'd obviously had a scare too, since she was actually encouraging Beehive to come inside. Beehive, on the other hand, was shaking her head.

"A nice strong cup of tea will make you feel better."

"No, thank you." Beehive headed for the steps,

153

one hand up to her face, shielding her half-stripped paint job.

She hurried down the steps, stumbling on her tall red heels as she went. "It's all right."

Mrs. Carnahan quirked her mouth in puzzlement and stroked Dooley's head as she watched her go. Then she shivered, as if just realizing how chilly it was. "Well, you girls may as well come in, anyway."

A spicy smell, like apple cake, filled the entryway. Dooley tugged Nellie toward the kitchen, apparently trailing the aroma.

Nellie followed him, but her mind felt restless. It was as if something was wrong—as if she was missing something, or forgetting something. She stopped, making Dooley jerk on the leash and Peggy bump into her.

"What?" Peggy said, as Nellie spun around to meet her confused face.

"When does a door-to-door salesperson ever turn down an invitation to come in?" Nellie demanded.

"When they're attacked by dogs," Peggy said, trying to step around her and follow Mrs. Carnahan.

"Oh, man!" Nellie pulled at Dooley.

"Come on, Dool, you smart dog. Excuse us, Mrs. Carnahan. I have to run out for a minute. I'll be right back. I'm sorry."

Nellie tugged at the door with one hand, and a reluctant Dooley with the other. The way he'd fallen all over Beehive—that half-scrubbed face—Beehive's reaction—all of it made a crazy kind of sense now.

She opened the door to a cold, damp breath of air that rustled the newspaper lying on the hall table. Dooley abandoned the scent of apple cake and plunged through the opening.

They crossed the porch. He skidded at the edge where blowing rain had made it slippery. He clattered down the steps, not running but pulling steadily at the leash, tail beating the air.

Nellie blinked at the raindrops that fell harder, catching her face. She looked up and down the street, but Dooley never hesitated.

"Oh please," she prayed as the dog pulled her to the right, "don't let her get away."

There were cars parked all along the street, but no sign of Beehive. Dooley towed her on .

"Okay, Dool, let's run!" If she was making a mistake, she'd be in trouble for a year. But she couldn't run as fast as Dooley, and she couldn't let Beehive get away.

Gulping air, she fumbled with his leash. When it came loose, he streaked ahead, barking like a happy beagle on the trail of a rabbit.

Dogs never forgot. Feed a dog today, and years later he'll greet you like a long-lost brother.

Even under all that ridiculous disguise, Dooley knew Sara Salera. The face he'd unearthed under the Sonora Sunset and towering orange hair wasn't some middle-aged widow, but a very young, dark-haired girl.

24

Finding Janie's Mother

Nellie ran, losing sight of the dog as he blasted around the corner. "Oh please," she kept praying. "Please, please."

She was violating the leash law, but she had no choice. Nellie's heart pounded. If only he stayed out of the street.

She spotted them just around the corner. Beehive was pushing him away, trying to get into her car. "Good Barney, good dog. Go away!"

Sara was sobbing. Dooley had his front end partway through the car door and his back end squirming in pure delight.

"Miss Salera!" Nellie called. "Please wait."

She saw the woman freeze momentarily, then shove harder at the persistent dog. "Go away!"

Nellie ran up to the car. Her eyes met Sara's.

"I've got to go." The woman's voice was raw and hoarse. Streaks of black and purple and turquoise spread down her cheeks from her eyes.

Dooley licked them away.

"Sara?" Nellie asked gently, pulling Dooley down.

Beehive shook her head. "You have the wrong person." She turned her face away from Nellie to fumble in her purse.

"I might," Nellie admitted. "But not Dooley. You can't fool a dog. They always know."

Sara buried her face in a wad of tissues and cried. Nellie had never heard anyone cry like that. It was an awful sound from the bottom of a troubled soul.

Shifting her wet feet awkwardly, Nellie reached out to pat Sara's shoulder. When the red-eyed woman looked up, Nellie was shocked. Her makeup washed away, she didn't seem much older than Jessica, or even Nellie.

"How did you know my name? I didn't tell anybody my name."

"You told the vet before Janie—I mean Liz-beth—was born."

Sara pulled off her wig and tossed it in the back. She closed her eyes and slumped in the seat. "The vet. I forgot. That was so stupid of me."

Nellie shivered as the wind changed direction. "Please come back to Mrs. Carnahan's."

Sara shook her head. She opened her eyes and looked at Nellie. "I can't," she pleaded. "I'll go away and not bother her. But I can't go back."

"For your daughter, Sara," Nellie urged her. "You owe her that much."

Sara just shook her head. "I can't raise her. I

can't do it. And I'm so awful. They'll put me in jail. What will that do to Lizbeth?" Her face was desperate. "I'm awful. I didn't mean to be, but I am."

Nellie shook her head. "I know you're not awful. Look how good you were to Dooley. And I know you love Lizbeth. You couldn't stay away from her, even when it meant you might get caught."

"No!" The word was explosive. "Do you know what I did to her?"

"Yes. But you can still change things. Please come back to Mrs. Carnahan's. She'll know what to do."

Seeming to recognize she had no choice, Sara picked up her purse and got out of the car. Dooley danced around her like a big-footed butterfly.

When they got back to Mrs. Carnahan's kitchen, Peggy was up to her elbows in warm apple cake. Mrs. Carnahan handed Lizbeth to Nellie and hurried to make tea.

Gently Nellie transferred the baby to Sara. Dooley sat with earnest attention, big drops of slobber clinging to his jaws. Nellie tossed him some cake crumbs.

"Who'd like to explain what's going on?" Mrs. Carnahan asked, pulling Lavar out of the cupboard, where he'd been rearranging her pots and pans.

Nellie started talking, telling what she knew, while Peggy's eyes got huge over a suspended forkful of cake. Sara cuddled her daughter, never looking up.

When Mrs. Carnahan brought the tea, she patted Sara's shoulder as if she was comforting a little kid and Sara ventured an upward glance. One look at the woman's sympathetic face brought a new flood of tears.

"Here, child, let me hold Janie while you sip that tea. It'll put the strength back into you."

After awhile, Sara had quieted to an occasional hiccuping breath. She held the tea cup in both hands, inhaling its fragrance.

"I've ruined both our lives," she said.

Mrs. Carnahan shook her head and poured more tea. "Seems to me you're a little young to have ruined your entire life."

Sara began to speak then, and to tell her own story. The summer before she'd started college, she'd had a waitress job and gotten involved with someone older who came into the restaurant. Her big sister had run off with somebody who'd turned out to be a real bum, and her parents were determined not to let Sara mess up her life that way.

Sara's parents didn't approve of the man she was seeing and said he was too old and might even be married for all she knew. They even locked her in her room. But Sara wouldn't listen.

Soon after she went away to college in Pittsburgh, he started coming to see her. The next thing she knew, she was going to have a baby. Telling this part made her blow her nose.

"Gary wanted me to get rid of it, but I—I just couldn't. I never heard from him again."

Unable to tell her strict parents, Sara decided to go away for a while until she could come home with her baby later as a "widow." She dropped out of school so she could earn some money. She made up a story about a French language work-study program in Canada. She arranged with a friend in the program to mail and receive letters for her. It was perfect, because the farmhouse where she was supposed to be staying had no phone.

To pay for her "summer program," her parents let her withdraw money from an education fund her grandmother had set up for her. They were only too happy to get her out of the country and away from her boyfriend. Everything seemed to be working out until Sara got a long-overdue letter from her parents by way of Quebec, telling her that her brother was about to take a job in Pittsburgh.

Sara couldn't take the chance of bumping into him, so she moved to Begg City. The rent was cheaper there, and she was able to work at a burger place for a couple months before the baby came.

It was a lonely life and pretty scary. "I got Barney, and it really helped, having someone else there with me. Dr. Mandelbaum boarded him for me when I went to the hospital in Pittsburgh to have my baby."

Sara reached for Lizbeth and held her close.

"It got awful after she was born. I do love her—I really do. But I was at the point where I wondered what was ever going to become of us. We couldn't live much longer like we were. I needed a job, and friends and—" Her voice caught.

"And Lizbeth never slept. It was just day and night with the crying and no sleep. The apartment was a mess; I was a mess—I couldn't even take a quick shower without that crying."

She drew a breath. "I just lost it. I never meant to hurt her, but I was so exhausted and my life felt like it was over, and I was just too rough with her."

When Jessica took the baby, Sara had panicked. "But when I calmed down, I realized it had to have been Jessica—that note, it had to be her. And I knew she'd take care of Lizbeth. All afternoon I was frantic, trying to decide what to do. What kind of mother doesn't even know if she should look for her missing child?" Her voice was full of self-disgust. "But if I went to the police, they'd arrest me.

"Then I saw the news. I saw the police and the foster care report, and I thought Lizbeth was better off. She was safe; she was taken care of; she could get a fresh start on life. If I showed up—" She stroked Lizbeth's head.

Nellie's chest felt tight. She looked at Peggy, who seemed to have lost her appetite for apple cake.

"I decided right then I had to get away—not too many people here knew me, but if I stayed, I was taking a chance. The people in my building would definitely notice that the baby wasn't crying and there weren't any diaper boxes in the dumpster anymore. I took Dooley to the shelter and told the building manager we were moving back to my hometown."

"But you didn't," Nellie said.

"No. I got as far as Greensburg. But then I had to see her. I had to know she was all right. But if I got caught—" Sara gulped and bit her lip.

"I was a theater major, so naturally I figured I'd just become someone else—a wig, some padding, different clothes, and makeup."

Different was definitely the word. "Where did you get the sample case?" Peggy asked. "It looks real."

"It is." Sara's lip curled in a half-smile. "I was going to sell the stuff last summer."

Dooley laid his chin on Sara's lap and sighed. "I let you down, too, bud," she admitted. She put her hand on his head and kissed Lizbeth. "God's going to punish me forever for what I did."

Nellie's heart twisted. "Oh, Sara, no. God doesn't work like that. God'll forgive you if you ask."

Sara's eyes looked far older than her smooth face. "It's not that easy to forgive myself."

25

A Thanksgiving Party

The youth group Thanksgiving party at Rick's house was a lot happier meeting than the previous one. Younger kids who didn't mind getting wet were bobbing for apples in the farm kitchen. Sounds of shrieking and splashing alternated with the good-natured rumble of Mr. Keppler's voice.

A mound of burgers, chips, salad, applesauce, and cake weighted down the big table in the dining room. All the older kids were lined up to fill their plates—all except Rick, Nellie, and Peggy, who were in a corner of the living room by the fireplace, waiting for the crowd to die down.

The fire crackled softly and spat sparks, casting leaping shadows on Rick's face. "What's going to happen to them?" he asked.

"The baby's staying with Mrs. Carnahan for now," Nellie said, answering the easy part. "Sara's free right now and she's getting counseling. Her lawyer's working on whatever comes next."

She lowered her voice. Kathy Bauer still insisted Sara should get a life sentence. Suzi tended to agree, but that seemed to be mostly because of the embarrassment she, her own sensitive self, had suffered following the babysitting disaster in the church basement.

"I don't think she's decided yet, whether or not to try to get the baby back. She said at first that Lizbeth would be better off adopted, but that's a big decision to just pop off and make."

"I wonder if she'd want to talk to me," Rick pondered out loud. "Maybe it would help to talk to a kid who was in her daughter's shoes once."

Nellie squeezed his hand. "I'll bet it would."

"At least she squared things with her parents," Peggy said. "I don't think they were exactly thrilled with the news, but now everything's out in the open and they're all talking to each other. And Mrs. Carnahan's getting to be like a big sister to her."

"I wish she could pray about it," Nellie said wistfully. "That's the only way things will really change for her."

"Well, we'll just have to keep doing it for her." Rick stood up as laughing kids with plates of food filed into the room. "We'd better get in there while there's something left besides an empty chip bag."

Later, as they all sat around the fire, someone suggested they provide babysitting during the upcoming Advent services.

"Feel free to count me out," Nellie said. "I've retired from babysitting—except for a certain member of my immediate family."

"Sorry!" Peggy echoed, putting both hands up in panic. "I'll help decorate the church or go caroling or something, but no more sitting."

Suzi shuddered. "Well, don't look at me. I already gave my all in the Great Babysitting Disaster." She scrambled up and headed for the dining room. "It'll be in all the encyclopedias someday, along with the San Francisco Earthquake, the Chicago Fire, and the Johnstown Flood—right next to *my* picture.'

" 'Next to *my* picture,' " Peggy simpered in soft imitation, making Nellie giggle.

"Big deal," Lou Cascio said, flexing a muscle. "What's a few little kids? The *men* will take care of it."

All around him, people started getting up and heading back to the food table. "Caroling sounds good to me," Rick said. "We can go to the nursing home."

"Maybe we have enough in the treasury to hire a babysitter," Ron suggested.

Nellie laughed. "Finally we have something this group can agree on!"

The Author

Soon after Susan Wright's family brought Newton home from the animal shelter, they knew he was a dog with a past. His whining and searching, whenever he heard loud voices or children crying, made them wonder where he'd come from. Although Newton's past remains an unsolved mystery, Susan used the incident in writing *Death by Babysitting*.

Susan was born in Somerset, Pennsylvania, and grew up in the mountains of western Pennsylvania. She loved mystery stories because wonderful and amazing things happened to ordinary people. Her two dreams were to be a writer and to own a black horse.

Susan later became a lawyer in Pittsburgh, but her dreams didn't go away. She now lives and writes in an old farmhouse on a country road, along with her husband, Dave, and three children—Tony (1984), Kika (1986), and Daisy

(1986). Besides Newton, their herd of livestock has grown to include Rufus—who arrived as a kitten with a broken leg—a hamster named Furball, Clarence the guinea pig, an abandoned white rabbit named Easter, and yes, a black horse named Nick.